D1057862

MARY ELIZABETH

Welcome to America!

MARY ELIZABETH
Welcome to America!

ELEANOR CLARK

HONOR ✠ NET
THE HONOR NETWORK

Dedication

TO MY GRANDCHILDREN AND GREAT grandchildren. May you recognize, love, and appreciate your rich Christian heritage and the privilege of living in America, which was founded on the trust and hope we have in Jesus. May you continue the legacy.

Contents

Acknowledgments

O MY LORD AND SAVIOR, JESUS CHRIST, who has blessed me with the greatest family, life, and country. May every word bring honor and glory to Your name.

To my publisher, Jake Jones, who recognized the potential of my stories and my heart's desire to bless and encourage young readers to value their American and Christian heritage.

To my writer, Janice Thompson, who understood my love of history and breathed life into my stories with the skill of her pen.

To Annabelle Meyers who helped develop the character lessons.

Blessed is the man that endureth temptation: for when he is tried, he shall receive the crown of life, which the Lord hath promised to them that love him.

—James 1:12

"While we have our tea today, I'm going to tell you a story about this little teapot," she explained. "It's been in our family for generations."

THE TEA PARTY

ENNIFER JEAN LEANED HER HEAD AGAINST the back seat of the car and sighed. "Mom, do I *have* to go to this tea party at Grand Doll's house?" she asked. Jennifer Jean thought of her grandmother who they lovingly called Grand Doll. She loved going to her grandmother's house, but she felt silly dressing up for a tea party. "Don't you think I'm too old for this?"

Her mom continued to drive, but with a smile she answered, "Oh, I don't know. Your grandmother always makes these parties so much fun for you girls. I think you'll have a great time."

Jennifer Jean looked down at the white gloves and pink dress she wore. "I just think it's so...*immature*. Pink dresses. White stockings. White shoes. White gloves. White hats." She pulled the straw hat from her head and tossed it on the car seat. "I'm eleven years old—not five. I feel like a big baby dressed like this. It's just plain...weird."

"I thought you loved your grandmother's tea parties." Her mom gave a little shrug. "And getting dressed up is half the fun."

Jennifer Jean groaned and rolled her eyes. "I'll just be glad when this day is over. I want to go to the mall with my friends."

"There will be plenty of time for that later," her mom said. "Today is all about family."

Jennifer Jean let out another groan. Spending the day with a bunch of chattering little girls would probably put her in a bad mood. To be honest, she didn't want to have any fun. Not now. Not with her parents going through a divorce. Not when she might have to move far away.

Jennifer Jean just wanted to be left alone to figure things out on her own. That wouldn't happen at a noisy, childish tea party.

Just about that time, the car turned onto her grand-mother's street. Even from this distance, she could see the cobblestone lane with an overarching canopy of trees that led to the large two-story home with its beautiful columns. She drew in a deep breath, and suddenly felt a little better. Something about Grand Doll's house always made her feel that way.

"Grand Doll and Poppie have the prettiest house in the world," Jennifer Jean said as she stretched to see out the window.

"Perfect for tea parties," her mom said with a wink.

Jennifer Jean wanted to say, "Whatever," but she knew her mom would be disappointed by her response. Truthfully, the last thing she wanted to do right now was to cause mama more pain. She was going through such a hard time already.

As the car turned into the driveway, a group of familiar little girls came running out the front door of the house. Seconds later Jennifer Jean climbed from the car and was greeted by her younger cousins.

Little Holly, blonde and bright-eyed, clutched a worn Raggedy Ann doll in her arms. "We're going to have so much fun!" she said as she bounced up and down in excitement.

Kimberly Dawn, nearly nine, nodded in agreement, and then showed off her newest doll. "She looks just like me, don't you think?" The doll did bear her resemblance, right down to the beautiful blonde hair. Jennifer Jean was secretly a little envious of her cousins with their light, golden hair.

"I hope Grand Doll doesn't make us eat crumpets and scones this time," Chelsea Marie, known to be a little stubborn, grumbled. "I want macaroni and cheese." As she clutched her ballerina doll and pouted, the sunlight seemed to capture the freckles on her face and bring them to life.

"Macaroni and cheese at a fancy tea party?" Grand Doll appeared at the front door with a wide smile on her face. "I think not!"

Jennifer Jean looked up at her grandmother and couldn't help but giggle. Grand Doll's lacy pink dress, as well as her white gloves and hat, made her look like one of the girls. From underneath the brim of her hat, her silvery-white curls glistened in the afternoon sunlight.

"See?" Jennifer Jean's mom leaned down and whispered in her ear. "I told you—Grand Doll always makes everything fun. Just go along with it, Honey. You'll have a great time."

The girls said good-bye to their moms who were leaving for a shopping expedition. Secretly, Jennifer Jean longed to go with them. Anything would be better than this. Instead, she gave a little shrug and entered the house with the others, who were chattering merrily.

"Let me have your invitations, please," Grand Doll said as she extended her hand.

Jennifer Jean's cousin, Rachel Ann, was the first to hand their grandmother her gold-embossed invitation. "Thank you for inviting me, Grand Doll," the pretty blonde said with a smile.

"You're very welcome."

Jennifer Jean shook her head. *How could Rachel Ann, who was ten years old, play along with such a silly game?*

Melanie Ann, who was even older, went next. She didn't seem to mind this childishness either.

Little Sara Elizabeth, only seven, batted her lashes across her dark brown eyes as she pressed her invitation into Grand Doll's hands. "I'm *so* happy to be here!" she exclaimed.

"And I'm *so* happy to have you!" Grand Doll responded with a little giggle.

One by one they handed in their invitations.

When they finished, their grandmother clapped her hands to get their attention. "I have a special surprise this year! Follow me." She led them to the sunroom at the back of the house, where they discovered a tiny table and small chairs. "Your dolls will have a tea party of their own this year." She gestured to the table, which was set with minia-ture teacups and saucers. A tiny teapot sat in the center of the table. Jennifer Jean couldn't help but wonder if it was filled with one of Grand Doll's flavored teas.

She shook her head as the others squealed in delight. *How silly to have a party for dolls.*

Still, the others seemed to like the idea. Her cousins went to work at once, setting their dolls in the various chairs. All but Jennifer Jean. Even Melanie Ann brought her doll, Baby Chrissie.

"Where is your doll, Jennifer Jean?" Grand Doll's fore-head wrinkled as she asked the question.

Jennifer Jean shrugged. "I packed my dolls away last year. I'm too old for them. I'm *eleven*."

"Nonsense." Grand Doll went at once to the back bedroom and came out with a beautiful cloth doll with a lovely porcelain face, dressed in a long, flowing gown. "Now you may join the others." She pressed the doll into Jennifer Jean's hands, who in turn placed the doll into the one remaining little chair.

"Now we're ready for our tea party!" Bits of sunlight peeked in through the window, causing Grand Doll's pink cheeks to practically glow as she talked. "Let's all say hello to your grandfather, Poppie, before we begin, shall we?"

They went into the den, and each girl gave their grandfather a hug. Jennifer Jean's heart ached as she looked at him, seated in the large leather recliner. Something about Poppie seemed different lately. Everyone said so. Mama said he was just getting forgetful, but why did he call Holly by a different name? And why did he look confused?

Grand Doll leaned over to kiss Poppie on his forehead. "If you need us, Dear, we'll be in the dining room," she told him. He nodded, and turned his attention back to the newspaper.

Jennifer Jean traipsed along behind the others as they made their way into the decorated dining room.

"Oh, Grand Doll, it's so pretty!" Melanie Ann giggled as she spun around for a glance at the room.

"Yes, it's be-u-tee-ful!" Holly added.

Jennifer Jean looked at the large mahogany table, covered with the elegant white tablecloth. It truly was a sight to behold. Eight place settings, each with beautiful china plates and cups. Eight lace napkins. Eight tall, crystal goblets for water. Tiny crystal vases with pink rosebuds peeked out in the center of the table, along with white flickering candles. Grand Doll certainly knew how to throw a party.

"Remove your hats and gloves, girls," their grandmother said. "And then look for your place cards."

Sure enough, each girl had her own place at the table. Jennifer Jean, happy to be rid of her hat and gloves, took her seat right next to Rachel Ann. Surely, by the end of this silly game, she would convince her cousin what nonsense this was.

Grand Doll stood at the head of the table and lifted a delicate white teapot with a rosebud on the side. "While we have our tea today, I'm going to tell you a story about this little teapot," she explained. "It's been in our family for generations."

"Generations?" Little Chelsea looked confused. "What's...*generations*?"

Grand Doll chuckled. "Let's just say this teapot has been in our family for many, many years. Does that make more sense?" Chelsea nodded.

Grand Doll poured tea into each girl's cup. "You'll notice that I used the Castleton Rose china," she explained. "It's my favorite. And the little demitasse cups are just right for a tea party, wouldn't you agree?"

"They're so cute!" Holly said as she held hers up in the air, almost spilling tea.

"Careful now," Grand Doll said. "Remember our manners." She went on to explain how all little girls should use proper manners at the table. She demonstrated how to use the silverware, and then went on to talk about the lace napkins with pink rosebuds, which she had the girls unfold and place on their laps.

Holding hers up, Grand Doll placed it to her mouth and said, "Little girls go *blot, blot.*" She dabbed at her pink lips to show them how.

"Blot, blot!" Sara Elizabeth's big brown eyes lit up as she tried it.

"Blot, blot!" Holly echoed.

Before long, all the girls practiced blotting their lips. All but Jennifer Jean, who secretly wished she could leave right now and go into the other room with Poppie. Surely he wouldn't make her go through this silliness. Besides, she needed someone to talk to today about her problems—her real problems.

"Come now, Jennifer Jean." Grand Doll gave her a curious look. "Blot like the others. Don't rub or you will muss your lipstick."

With a sigh, she picked up her napkin and pretended to blot her lips.

"Now then," Grand Doll said as she placed her napkin back on the table, "it's time to say grace."

All the girls bowed their heads, and their grandmother offered thanks for the food.

Afterwards, Grand Doll lifted her head and smiled. "Time to eat!" She served up tiny, crustless sandwiches, cut into fancy diamond shapes.

"What are they?" Chelsea Marie's nose wrinkled as she picked up one to examine it. "They look icky."

"Now, now," Grand Doll scolded, "they're yummy. Cream cheese with dill. I made them just for this occasion."

"Mmm." That did sound good, and Jennifer Jean was a little hungry. Perhaps she could bear this long enough to eat with the others before excusing herself to go into the other room for some privacy.

"Can't we have macaroni and cheese?" Chelsea let out a little groan, and the others giggled.

"Not today," Grand Doll explained. "Today we're having a tea party, just as they would have had back in the days when our relatives first came to America almost 400 years ago. And I'm serving your tea out of the very teapot they would have used."

Now Kimberly Dawn's eyes grew large. "No way!"

"Way."

"Grand Doll," Jennifer Jean couldn't help but ask, "are you saying that teapot is almost four hundred years old?"

"It is."

"Wow." Jennifer Jean could hardly believe it.

Grand Doll's eyes lit up as she explained. "You remember the memory trunk, don't you?"

All the girls nodded, including Jennifer Jean. For as long as she could remember, Grand Doll had told them stories about the big, black trunk in the garage that was filled with items from years gone by.

"The teapot came from the trunk, along with several other items I'm going to share with you today. I have quite a story to tell, so I hope you all have your listening ears on today."

Jennifer Jean wasn't sure if she was in the mood for a story or not, but it would probably be better than a tea party.

"What's this, Grand Doll?" Sara Elizabeth held up a tiny crystal rolling pin.

"Oh, that's to rest your knife on, so it won't get the tablecloth dirty." Grand Doll went on to talk about some of the other pretty items on the table—the little crocheted "booties" that held their crystal goblets, which she explained were made by her Aunt Augie years ago, and the "Lily of the Valley" silverware, which Poppie had given Grand Doll for their twenty-fifth wedding anniversary.

Before long, everyone was nibbling at their sandwiches and chattering away. Jennifer Jean got so busy talking with the others that she almost forgot *not* to have fun. Almost.

After their sandwiches, Grand Doll reached for a plate of yummy-looking scones.

"Mmm, my favorite!" Rachel Ann licked her lips in preparation.

Their grandmother served the scones and some little tea cakes too, and then asked if anyone would like more tea.

Jennifer Jean nodded. "I would, please."

Grand Doll came around her way with the teapot in hand, and whispered in her ear, "Having a good time, Jennifer Jean?" She offered up a nod, realizing that she really was having fun—whether she'd meant to or not.

As they nibbled at the yummy scones and tea cakes and sipped from warm cups of tea, Grand Doll seemed to grow more serious. The other girls didn't seem to notice. They played with their teacups, setting their spoons across the top of their saucers, just as their grandmother had taught them to do in years past.

All but Jennifer Jean. She knew Grand Doll well, and could sense a story coming. That's why she wasn't surprised by her grandmother's next words.

"Girls, I think it's time I told you the story of the teapot. Would you like to hear it now?"

They all began to squeal at once. Grand Doll smiled as she lifted the delicate china teapot and began the story she had promised them.

Her mother and father spoke of a new life in America—a wonderful life filled with excitement and adventure.

SETTING SAIL
ENGLAND 1635

ARY ELIZABETH, ARE YE NEARLY ready, child? We'll be leaving soon." Ten-year-old Mary Elizabeth looked up from the doll she'd been playing with into her mother's excited face.

"But we've been traveling for weeks already, Mam," the youngster said, using the Welsh term for mother. "Won't we *ever* get to Virginia?"

A smile graced her mother's lips. "Oh, Darling," she said, "our journey has barely begun. We've only just come from Wales to Scotland and then England. Most of our travels from this point onward will be aboard a big ship called the *Assurance*, sailing all the way to America. That will take weeks, child. Weeks."

"Weeks?" Mary Elizabeth didn't feel like traveling for weeks. To be honest, all she wanted to do was go back home again, to Wales, to play with her best friend, Alva. At the very thought of Alva, tears came to her eyes. *When would she ever see her dearest friend in the world again, or would they be separated forever?*

"It's not fair," she whispered. "It's not."

Still, she had to go. Her mother and father spoke of a new life in America—a wonderful life filled with excitement and adventure. They would have plenty of land. They could grow crops and get to know new neighbors. Most importantly, they could worship God freely, without fear. And that, according to her father, was the best reason of all for leaving everything they had known and loved to travel across the ocean to a new life.

"I'll miss my *old* life," Mary Elizabeth whispered again.

She would miss their town of Laugharne. She would miss standing atop the hillside and looking across the meadow at the beautiful Laugharne Castle. She would miss long walks with her beloved father—whom she and her brother lovingly called *Tad*—along the shoreline of Carmathen Bay. Most of all, she would miss the sound of Alva's laughter ringing out across the fields as they played together on lazy summer afternoons.

What she would not miss were the winters, cold and frigid. A little shiver rippled down Mary Elizabeth's back as she remembered the freezing temperatures this past January. Perhaps America would be a warm place, a place without snow or ice. She hoped so, anyway.

At that moment, her father appeared at the door. "*Ma-ree*, you darling girl!" he exclaimed.

She looked up with new excitement. How she loved the singsongy way her name sounded as it rolled across her father's tongue—almost like music.

"Tad, you look so handsome in your traveling clothes."

"Thank ye, Dearie."

She gazed at him in admiration. She loved his wavy brown hair and neatly trimmed moustache. They made him appear quite gentlemanly.

"The ship sails in just a few hours. The captain has blown the horn. Passengers are boarding, even now. We must be on our way."

"We're sailing on a big ship!" Mary Elizabeth's seven-year-old brother, Liam, did a little jig, making everyone laugh. His light brown curls bounced up and down with each fanciful step.

"Aye, we're sailing on a big ship," their father said with a smile. "But the ship will sail without the Powell family if we don't hurry along, and that would be a shame. So come along with me, everyone." At this point, Tad broke into an old Welsh song about sailing across the waters. His voice, rich and strong, put a smile on Mary Elizabeth's face. Before long, everyone sang along.

As her father and the others gathered up the bags, Mary Elizabeth looked around the room of the inn one last time and wondered if she would ever return to

England again. Perhaps one day, but for now she would board the ship and travel to Virginia. Uncle Gaynor, Tad's younger brother, was already there, waiting for them. When they arrived, he would help them build their new home.

"Virginia," Mary Elizabeth whispered, letting the word roll off her lips. If the place was half as pretty as its name, it was bound to be beautiful. Soon, hopefully very soon, she would see for herself.

Mary Elizabeth gripped her little rag doll, the one she had lovingly named Alva, in her hands. The pretty doll had a lovely Dresden china face, and her brown hair looked a bit like Alva's. So did her smile, though it was painted on a bit crooked. Still, holding the doll in her hands made Mary Elizabeth miss her friend a little less.

Almost an hour later, the entire Powell family stood at the harbor, gazing up at the beautiful *Assurance* with its massive white sails.

"Oh, Tad!" Mary Elizabeth marveled. "She's a big one!"

"She is, indeed."

"Are we really going aboard?" Liam turned toward his father, eyes wide.

"We are," Tad answered. Then he turned his attention to the large trunks filled with their belongings. "First I need to locate someone to help us with our things."

Mary Elizabeth gazed down at the largest trunk, a big black one. She knew it contained many of the family's most cherished possessions—her mother's favorite teapot, her grandmother's hand-tatted tablecloth, and even her great grandfather's wax seal with the family crest.

Others nearby loaded many of their possessions as well. Mary Elizabeth looked about and saw large pieces of furniture, farming tools, and the like.

As a man came to load their trunks, Mary Elizabeth's mother gave him a polite nod. "Take care with this one, kind sir," she said. "If you don't mind."

"Of course." He offered a nod and then went to work, loading the trunks.

"Hold my hands, children." Mam extended both hands. Mary Elizabeth tucked her doll under her arm as she took hold of her mother's right hand. Liam took hold of the left. The Powell family wound their way through the throng of people until they reached the large gangplank. Tad led the way with a whistle on his lips.

Liam's eyes were wide as they walked up, up, up the wooden plank to the entrance of the ship, where Tad met with one of the crewmen.

"Heading to the colonies, are ye?" the happy-go-lucky fellow asked.

"Indeed," Tad said proudly, his shoulders and head held high. "My brother has gone ahead of us and acquired a piece of land in Virginia."

The fellow nodded as he answered. "Virginia. I've been there, me-self. Beautiful place. I wish ye the best." He glanced down at their tickets once more. "Cabins are mid-deck."

"Many thanks to ye," Tad said with a big smile.

The ship was packed full of passengers—some dressed nicely, others wearing worn, dirty clothes. Mary Elizabeth had never seen so many people together in one place before. She could scarcely breathe, with so many pressing in around her, and the smell was awful. Her stomach felt sick right away.

Tad lifted Liam onto his shoulders so the lad could see above the crowd. "What do ye think, son?" he called out.

"It's wonderful, Tad!" Liam exclaimed. "Can we live here?"

"Live on a ship?" Mam argued. "I dare say ye will be ready to leave this ship in less than a week, and wishing for dry land, I guarantee."

"Oh no, not me," Liam argued. "I was born to sail the seas."

"Oh, ye were, were ye?" Tad erupted in laughter, and Mary Elizabeth couldn't help but join in. "Well, I hope ye are seaworthy, my boy, for we'll be aboard this ship for many, many weeks."

"Many weeks?" Mary Elizabeth wasn't as sure of herself as Liam. She didn't want to stay aboard for many days, let alone many weeks. She just wanted to go back home again.

In just a few minutes they located their cabin. It was a tiny place, and dirty too.

"What is that smell?" Mam asked, pinching her nose.

"I couldn't begin to guess," Tad answered with a sour look on his face.

"Oh, Mam!" Mary Elizabeth said with a groan, "'tis awful!"

As they entered, Mam pulled off her cap and fluffed up her brown curls with her fingertips. Mary Elizabeth couldn't help but think her mother looked as regal as a queen, even in her simple blue dress.

"Welcome to your temporary home," Tad exclaimed. He looked around with a shrug. "Not exactly a castle, to be sure. But at least we're all together in one place."

Mam looked around with a frown on her face. "It's not the tidiest place I've ever seen, to be sure."

"Wherever will we all sleep?" Mary Elizabeth asked.

"And what will we eat?" Liam wanted to know.

"We will manage," Tad said, placing the small trunk with their provisions on the floor. "There will be plenty to eat, son, though not the usual fare."

"What then, Tad?" Liam asked.

"We've packed salted beef and dried fish," Tad explained, "and plenty of vegetables. Mam has baked several loaves of bread, a lot of biscuits, and we've got plenty of butter and jam."

"But what will we do while we're aboard ship?"

"We will sing songs," Tad said with a grin, "and play games, and tell stories. 'Twill be fun, to be sure!"

"Aye," Mam said with a smile. "We will make it fun, and hopefully the time will pass quickly. Before ye know it, we'll be in Virginia, and there will be plenty to do."

"Virginia." Mary Elizabeth said the word again. It became more real each time she spoke it.

Liam bounced up and down. "May I look about?" he asked. "Please?"

"You'll not be leaving this room without us, understood?" Mam's face grew tight as she spoke. "Too many dangers about. You will stay with your family and no arguments about it."

"Yes Mam." He shrugged his shoulders, and then took a seat upon the makeshift bed.

"We've no window," Mary Elizabeth said as she looked around the room.

"That's because we're mid-ship," Tad explained, "but never ye mind that. There will be plenty of time to see the waters from the deck. Just ye wait, darling girl!" he said, his blue eyes almost dancing with excitement. "This journey across the sea will be one ye will tell your children about. And your grandchildren. It will be an adventure like no other."

"Better than a visit to Laugharne Castle?" Liam quizzed.

"Far better." Tad nodded.

"Better than a walk alongside Carmathen Bay?" Mary Elizabeth asked.

Tad laughed. "By far, by far." His eyes took on a dreamy look as he spoke. "Children, we're about to head across the Atlantic Ocean. It's larger than any bay ye've ever seen in your life. Larger than a hundred bays. A thousand bays, even."

"Are ye jesting, Tad?" Liam asked. "A thousand bays?"

Mam chuckled. "As I said before, ye will wish the Atlantic was smaller than a pond by next week. This adventure will likely get a bit tiresome in no time a'tall."

"Now, now." Tad gave her a wink. "None of that. There'll be no complaining from the Powells on this trip. Singing, yes. Complaining, no." His smile lit up the cabin, and the singing began again.

Before long the whole family joined in. They sang of days gone by in Wales. And then they sang of new beginnings—in a place called Virginia.

They made their way up to the deck,
and Mary Elizabeth looked about in
wonder. "Oh, Tad! How exciting."

OUT TO SEA

HE FIRST DAY ABOARD THE SHIP WAS
filled with adventure. The rocking back
and forth as the *Assurance* set out to
sea. The exciting stories Tad told about their new home
in Virginia. It was all wonderful.

However, by the next morning, the trouble began for
Mary Elizabeth and her little brother.

"I don't feel good, Mam." Liam clutched his stomach,
his face looking a bit green.

"I am a bit off-kilter myself," Mary Elizabeth agreed.
In truth, she felt just awful. Her stomach ached, and she
felt dizzy and headachy, and the room, which had always
felt small, seemed even smaller than ever. The walls
seemed to be closing in around her. "I feel a bit like those
fish out there in the ocean. Everything inside of me is
swimming."

"Hmm." Tad reached to put his palm on her forehead.
"No fever." He stepped back to give the children a second

look. "I've a mind to think seasickness has taken hold of both of ye."

"Seasickness?" Mary Elizabeth asked, clutching her stomach. "The sea makes us sick?"

"Aye." Mam nodded. "Sometimes people don't take well to traveling upon the high seas. Might take a few days till your stomachs settle down."

She had no sooner spoken than Liam bolted from his seat, hands across his belly. He became sick right away. Just a few minutes later, Mary Elizabeth felt queasy and became sick as well. She moaned and groaned, feeling worse by the minute.

"Pray for me, Mam!" she cried out. "'Tis awful!"

At once her mother came to her side and began to pray aloud. Over and over the sickness came, until Mary Elizabeth was completely worn out.

Both children spent the next three days in bed, neither one holding down a bit of food, though Mam tried to feed them bits of dry toast and warm tea. The ship continued to rock back and forth, back and forth. Mary Elizabeth wanted nothing more than to turn the *Assurance* around and head back home. In fact, she didn't care if she never saw another ship again—as long as she lived.

All the while, she held onto her doll and moaned. "When will this end?" she cried out. "I can't bear another minute."

"Please, Tad," Liam begged. "Please take us home. I don't want to go to America. I just want to put my feet on dry land again."

"I'm inclined to agree," Mam was overheard to whisper.

Tad shook his head. "Nonsense, Powell family! We're made of tougher stuff than this. The seasickness will pass, and we will walk about on the deck and have a grand time. Why, I've half a mind to head out to the deck now to see who's about."

"Really?" Liam sat up in the bed. "Could I come along?"

"Perhaps tomorrow," Mam agreed. "If ye and your sister are feeling better, we'll sit out on the deck and watch the men working. In the meantime, let's pray for this sickness to pass." She bowed her head and prayed at length, asking the Almighty to spare her children from the sickness caused by the rocking of the ship.

Thankfully, the next morning Mary Elizabeth awoke hungry and healthy. "I'm starved!" she announced.

"Me too!" Liam echoed.

They dressed, and Mam fed them a breakfast of hardened biscuits and jam, along with large cups of lukewarm tea. "Go easy, children," she said. "If ye eat too much too fast, it'll come back to visit ye, for sure!"

Mary Elizabeth slowly nibbled the biscuit, wishing they were home again so she could have one of Mam's hot fluffy biscuits instead of this cold hard one. Still, she didn't complain. She wouldn't dare, not when Mam and Tad had sacrificed so much to make this trip possible.

"Are the Powells ready to go up to the deck?" Tad asked. "It's a sight to behold up there. Folks milling about, men hoisting sails and swabbing the deck, people singing and having a fine time."

"Oh yes, let's!" Mam agreed. "Sounds splendid!"

They made their way up to the deck, and Mary Elizabeth looked about in wonder. "Oh, Tad! How exciting."

Mam didn't look convinced. "It's dreadfully windy out here," she said, pulling a scarf over her hair. "I hope the children don't take sick again. And many of these people don't look happy a'tall."

Mary Elizabeth looked about. True, many of the people wore troubled expressions, but quite a few appeared to be taking the voyage well.

"We'll be fine, Mam!" Liam tugged at her hand. "I promise."

"As if the lad could make such a promise!" Tad said with a laugh. "We Powells are of strong constitution. We persevere through every trial, we do, and I believe the boy has spoken right. He will be healthy for the rest of the trip. The good Lord will see to it."

Just then, something caught Mary Elizabeth's attention. "Do you taste that, Mam?" she asked. "The air tastes like…like salt!" She leaned back and stuck out her tongue, just to make sure.

"It does!" Liam's tongue waggled back and forth, and then he turned to face his father with a curious look on his face. "Why, Tad?"

Their father laughed. "It's the saltwater from the ocean spraying up in your face, is all," he explained. "Imagine if ye worked aboard the ship, like so many of these men do. I hear the sailors have salt in their veins!"

"Salt in their veins?" Liam's eyes grew wide.

"Tad is teasing, Son." Mam patted him on the shoulder. "He has a fine sense of humor, to be sure."

Their father gave her a wink, and they headed off on their walk toward the front of the ship. Back and forth the boat rocked. Mary Elizabeth was pitched to and fro, and reached to clutch her mother's hand to remain steady.

She passed a young man whose skin was dark and leathery from the sun. He mopped the decks as they walked by.

"They call it 'swabbing' the decks," Tad reminded her.

Still, whatever they called it, mopping wasn't much fun, especially when you were tilting to and fro. Mary Elizabeth wondered how the poor fellow managed. Besides, it seemed no matter how hard he worked, the ship still appeared dreadfully dirty, and the smell just got worse by the day.

As they walked along through the crowd, the sound of a man singing rang out from above. His voice seemed to bounce against the wind:

Of all the trades in England, a-beggin' is the best
For when a beggar's tired, he can lay him down and
*   rest.*
And a-beggin' I will go, and a-beggin' I will go,
And a-beggin' I will go, and a-beggin' I will go.

"Mam, do ye hear him?" Mary Elizabeth looked up in awe. "I've never heard that song before. Have ye?"

"Never heard it, Miss?" the man hollered down. "Then let me entertain ye a bit longer!" He dove into it again, this time singing with gusto:

I sleep beneath the hollow trees, and there I pay no
*   rent.*
Providence provides for me, and I am well content.
And a-beggin' I will go, and a-beggin' I will go,
And a-beggin' I will go, and a-beggin' I will go.

The man's face lit into the biggest smile Mary Elizabeth had ever seen. He tipped his hat before he went back to work hoisting the sails.

"Mam," she whispered, "do you suppose he's really a beggar man?"

"Shush, child. Of course he's not. He's just a happy fellow, singing to pass the time as he works."

"Singing to pass the time?" Tad turned back to face them. "Is that a request, Mrs. Powell? Are ye asking me to sing for ye, now?"

"Well, Mr. Powell," she said with a sly grin, "if ye've a mind to sing, I've no cause to stop ye."

Mary Elizabeth couldn't help but giggle as Tad began to sing, almost as loud as the man above.

Lavender's blue, diddle diddle
Lavender's green,
When I am king, diddle diddle
You shall be queen.

Tad bowed in Mam's direction at the word "queen," and her cheeks turned pink.

"Blessings on ye, kind sir," she exclaimed. "I'll be your queen, thank ye very much!"

"And a fine one, at that!" He kissed the back of her hand and began to sing once again.

After a few more verses, he stopped singing and wrapped her in his arms, planting a little kiss on her forehead. Mary Elizabeth blushed, and then looked about to see if others were watching. Sure enough, an elderly woman with a sour look on her face glanced their way.

"Mr. Powell!" Mam scolded. "Not in front of the children."

"And why ever not?" he asked as he turned to face Mary Elizabeth and her brother. "I want them to know that I adore their Mam. Any harm in that?"

Mary Elizabeth giggled again, but Liam hid his face in his mother's skirt.

"Now see what ye've gone and done," Mam said with a sigh. "Ye've embarrassed the poor child."

"Nonsense." Tad lifted Liam onto his shoulders and began to sing again as they continued their walk. All the way from one end of the ship to the other, Mary Elizabeth enjoyed the sound of her father's singing, rising out above the crashing of the waves and the voices of the others they passed. Somehow, hearing his rousing voice lifted her spirits and made this dreadful voyage a little easier to take.

She looked about, wondering how the other passengers were faring. Surely many of them had been sick as well, and others were probably longing for home. She passed by a little girl clinging to her mother's skirts. The youngster looked frightened and pale. At about that time, they passed a young man about Liam's age, who waved and smiled.

"See, there are nice people aboard," her brother said with a smile.

"Indeed." Mary Elizabeth continued to look at the people, marveling at the clothes many of them wore. Surely the *Assurance* was filled to the brim with people from every country—and it showed in their dress. It showed in their language as well. She'd never heard so many different languages going at once. At times it sounded like a heavenly choir, one voice on top of the other. At other times it sounded like several instruments warming up just before a big performance.

Finally, just as they were about to return to their cabin, a little girl about Mary Elizabeth's age came into view. The youngster wore a pretty white dress, and had blonde curls. She smiled in their direction.

"May I say hello, Mam?" Mary Elizabeth whispered.

"Of course, Darling!"

She took a step in the direction of the girl and made introductions.

"Good day, and how ye be? I'm Mary Elizabeth Powell."

"I'm Abigail Morgan." The girl's blonde curls blew about in the wind. "But I go by Abby."

"Abby." Mary Elizabeth loved the sound of it.

"Where are you from?" Abby asked.

"Wales."

"Wales! I've a cousin in Wales," Abby exclaimed. "I'm from England."

"Aye. I could have guessed from your voice."

Abby chuckled. "And I could have guessed you were from Wales. Isn't that funny?"

Before long, the two girls were laughing and talking as if they had been friends forever. Mam and Tad struck up a conversation with Abby's parents, Mr. and Mrs. Morgan, and quickly learned that the family would be settling in Virginia, just like the Powells.

Abby's older sister, Hope, was a beautiful girl with long, golden-colored hair and soft pink cheeks. She smiled a lot, and many of the fellows aboard the ship turned their heads to give her another look as she went by. Mary Elizabeth didn't know when she had ever seen anyone more beautiful than Hope.

"Do you suppose we'll be neighbors?" Abby asked, her eyes growing wide. "I need a friend!"

"Oh, me too!" Mary Elizabeth could hardly believe it. Would they really be "forever friends" like she and Alva had hoped to be?

The sunlight streamed down from above, and the sound of laughter rang out across the deck as new friends got acquainted. For the first time since leaving home, Mary Elizabeth truly believed that traveling to America could very well turn out to be a great adventure, after all.

"The prettiest beach I've ever seen,"
Abby agreed. "The sand is whiter than
snow! Look—it goes on for miles!"

BARBADOS

*A*LL ASHORE THAT'S GOING ASHORE!"
The captain's booming voice rang
out. Mary Elizabeth gripped the
railing and looked overboard. She could hardly wait to
get off the ship. The voyage had been filled with hard
times, particularly the last few weeks. Many aboard
the *Assurance* had taken sick. Mam said it was because
so many people were living so close together. Most of
the ones who had smiled in the first few days now had
somber looks on their faces. Mary Elizabeth tried to
maintain a cheerful attitude, but it was hard.

Perhaps the most difficult of all—there was a stench
aboard the ship that all the swabbing in the world never
seemed to take away. The smell grew worse every day.
And the queasiness in her stomach had returned as the
smell grew stronger.

Now, as the passengers prepared to leave the ship, Mary Elizabeth tugged at her mother's skirt. "Are we in Virginia, Mam?"

"Not yet, Darling."

"We must be there," Liam argued. "I cannot abide one day more on this boat."

"Truly, Son?" Tad said with a grin. "Where is the little boy who claimed that he could live forever aboard the *Assurance*?"

Liam pouted, then took Tad's hand. "I was wrong."

"If we're not in Virginia," Mary Elizabeth said, "where are we?"

Mam squinted and put her hands over her eyes to shade herself from the bright sun above. "We've stopped for a spell on an island called Barbados."

"Barbados." With the sunlight streaming against her cheeks, Mary Elizabeth looked over the railing of the ship to the beautiful white shoreline. The hot afternoon sun caused the sand to glisten, almost making the beach look like her mother's strand of pearls. "What a lovely name for such a lovely place." She squinted and tried to take it all in at once.

"Beaches as far as the eye can see!" Tad said. "And underground lakes and caves, from what I've been told."

"May we see them?" Liam's eyes widened at the possibility.

"No caves for the Powell family," Mam scolded. "We'll head ashore for a few hours, and then board the ship for several more days at sea."

Mary Elizabeth couldn't help but groan. "More days at sea? Oh Mam, I'm weary with rocking back and forth, back and forth. I just want to put my feet on solid ground again. And the ship is filthy."

"It smells too," Liam said, not looking as happy as the first day they'd come aboard, to be sure.

"Well then," Tad said with a smile. "Just ye wait till we go ashore. Getting your land legs back might prove to be a bit of a problem."

"Land legs?" Mary Elizabeth looked up at him curiously. "What are land legs?"

"You will see." That's all he would say, but he did give her a little wink. "Come, Powell family. We've things to see, so stay close by at all times." He led the way toward the gangplank, where the island came into full view.

"Oh Tad!" Mary Elizabeth exclaimed. "It's so breezy and warm, and by far the prettiest place in all the world. May we just live here, in Barbados?"

"No, darling girl," he explained. "'Tis a lovely place, but I've no doubt ye will find Virginia to be even lovelier...though not as sandy, to be sure. Besides..." he leaned in to whisper, "I hear tell the island is filled with ruffians."

"Ruffians?" She echoed the word. "What are *ruffians*?"

"Men who are up to no good," he explained. "Misfits. Gamblers." Tad's eyes grew large.

"I've even heard tell there are buccaneers about," Mr. Morgan's voice rang out as Mary Elizabeth turned to find their new friends standing directly behind them.

She wanted to ask what a buccaneer was, but the voices of the crowd grew so loud, she could scarcely hear herself think. Instead, she reached to take hold of Abby's hand, so they could enjoy this adventure together.

"This way, Powell family!" Tad's voice rose above the noise as he made his way onto the gangplank, tipping his hat at the captain as they left the ship.

"This way, Morgan family!" Mr. Morgan echoed.

"Stay together, children." Mary Elizabeth's Mam called out, as she looked around with concern in her eyes.

Mary Elizabeth clung to Abby's hand and tried to keep up with their parents, but her legs felt all wobbly. In fact, she almost felt as if she were still aboard the ship, tipping this way and that.

As the family finally came upon a quiet spot, Tad turned to face them all. "Got your land legs yet, Powells, or are ye still a bit shaky?"

Liam squatted down and then stood again. "My legs have turned to jelly, Tad!"

"And I'm a bit shaky as well," Mary Elizabeth explained. "How long will it last?"

"A few hours perhaps," Mr. Morgan answered.

"Hours?" Abby questioned. "I'm not sure I can bear it."

"Give it some time, little sister," Hope said with a smile. "Before you know it, you will be good as new."

"Fortunately, we don't have far to go." Tad pointed at the white sand and smiled. "How do the Powell children feel about an afternoon in the sunshine with waves lapping at your feet?"

"Really?" Liam squealed. "May we go into the water?"

Tad nodded, and moments later they walked across the shoreline to the edge of the waves.

"Only up to your knees," Mam said with a stern look. "Remember, Liam, you're not a strong swimmer."

Mary Elizabeth stared out at the waves, which rolled in one on top of the other. The white spray at the top of the water looked a bit like frosting on a cake. "Oh, Abby, it's so beautiful," Mary Elizabeth said, looking up with a smile.

"The prettiest beach I've ever seen," Abby agreed. "The sand is whiter than snow! Look—it goes on for miles!"

"Indeed!"

"Dip your toes in the clear blue Caribbean Sea," Tad suggested.

Mary Elizabeth quickly loosened her shoes and pulled them from her feet. She could hardly wait to stick her feet into the water. *Would it be cold like Carmathen Bay back at home in Wales?* she wondered.

"Liam, come with me!" She took her brother by the hand and they ran to the water's edge. He squealed with delight as the waves lapped over their toes.

"Ooo! It's warm!" Mary Elizabeth looked at her Mam with joy. "So very warm! Join us, Mam!"

"Oh, I mustn't."

"Why mustn't ye?" Tad asked, as he sat in the sand to pull off his shoes. "I dare say ye will not be passing this way again. So let's dip our toes into the Caribbean Sea, Mrs. Powell. We'll have a dandy time of it."

Mary Elizabeth giggled with glee as Tad and Mam joined them at the waters edge. There, along with the Morgan family, they played in the warm waves for more than an hour.

The sound of another ship pulling up to the dock caught the family's attention. Mary Elizabeth looked up in time to see a group of people coming down the gangplank of the large wooden vessel—their arms and legs bound with chains. They had the darkest skin she had ever seen, and the women wore their hair tightly coiled. And none of them looked happy. Not at all, in fact.

"Mam?" Mary Elizabeth turned, curious. "Who are they?"

"Yes, and why do they look so sad?" Abby asked.

Tad stared off in the distance. "Ah. That ship is from Africa."

A look of concern came in Mam's eyes. "I've heard tell of this, but never seen it for myself. How dreadful!"

"What is it, Mam?" Mary Elizabeth asked.

Her mother just shook her head and turned the other way.

"Those people have been brought to Barbados to work as slaves," Mr. Morgan whispered.

"Slaves?" Liam looked up, clearly confused. "What's a slave?"

"Yes," Mary Elizabeth wondered aloud, "And why did they have to be brought? Didn't they want to come?"

Tad shook his head, but didn't answer right away. "It's a hard question you're asking Dearie." He gave Mr. Morgan a sad look, and the two men grew silent.

Mary Elizabeth looked at the people one more time as they grew closer. "Why are their hands and feet bound?" she asked.

Mam didn't answer, but her face grew quite serious. Hope dabbed at her eyes and looked the other way.

One of the men must have angered the fellow in charge, because he brought out a whip and lashed the poor man across the back several times.

Mary Elizabeth let out a scream. "Oh, Tad." She buried her face in her hands. "They're so mean. Why must they beat him?" She wondered if, perhaps, the man with the whip in his hand was a buccaneer, like Tad had said.

"It's a fretful thing, indeed," her father said as he swept her into his arms. "There are a great many things we won't understand in this life, Darling, and I'm afraid ye've just witnessed one of them."

"There are so many tragedies around us," Mrs. Morgan said softly. "Conditions aboard our ship, the *Assurance,* are deplorable. Did you hear about that little boy who died? I heard it might have been from smallpox."

"Smallpox?" Mam's eyes grew large. "I hadn't heard about that, but I have heard rumors about a measles epidemic."

"Yes," Mrs. Morgan added. "Those unfortunate people have been quarantined below deck. Can you imagine what it must smell like down there? As bad as it is on our deck, it must be dreadful down below." She fanned her face.

Mam shook her head in disbelief. "'Tis a shame we must all go through this, but the good Lord will see us through. I know He will. I am thankful for His blessings and protection upon us."

"Yes," Mrs. Morgan agreed. "Though, I, for one, will be happy to see this voyage come to an end soon. There's so little to do aboard the ship. The children grow weary and bored. And...," she leaned in to whisper the rest, though Mary Elizabeth could still hear her, "I understand some on board have gone a bit stir-crazy, stirring up trouble with one another."

"Aye," Mam said. "I've heard tell of a few incidents. My dear babes have witnessed far more hardships over these past several weeks than in all the years we lived in Wales. Sometimes it makes me wonder…"

She stopped short of finishing her sentence, but Mary Elizabeth had to wonder if Mam didn't question why they had left Wales in the first place. To be honest, she still wondered. Sometimes, anyway.

Just then the ship let out several loud horn blasts.

"I believe it's time for the Powells to go aboard once again," Tad said.

"And the Morgans as well," Mr. Morgan added.

They all brushed the sand from their feet and fastened their shoes, then headed back to the *Assurance* where a crowd of people waited to board together. At the foot of the gangplank, vendors sold a variety of foods—bananas, mangoes, and even a little round fruit Mary Elizabeth had never seen before. She reached to pick one up and rolled it around in her palm.

"What is it?" she asked Mam.

"It's a kiwi," Mr. Morgan explained, "and I hear they are quite tasty."

"It all looks so wonderful," Mrs. Morgan said. "May we buy some?"

"Perhaps," her husband agreed, "but we won't purchase much, my dear. It's sure to spoil after a few days aboard the ship."

Both of the families purchased a few fresh fruits and vegetables and then began to board. Just as they entered the ship, Mary Elizabeth looked back at the African slaves, with their ankles and wrists bound with chains. Her heart nearly broke. She wanted to reach out to hug them. She wanted to remove their chains. She wanted to tell them that everything would be just fine, but she couldn't.

Later that night, Mary Elizabeth settled into her warm bed in the cabin, but she couldn't stop thinking about the people she had seen along the white sands of the shore of Barbados. In truth, she wondered if she would ever forget their sad faces as long as she lived.

"What can I do for them, Lord?" she whispered.

Suddenly an idea came. Though she couldn't help them directly, she could pray for them. With a heavy heart, she lifted a prayer heavenward.

"Welcome to America, Mary Elizabeth!" he exclaimed. "Welcome to your new home!"

AMERICA!

"MAM, IS THAT IT? IS THAT REALLY, really it?" Mary Elizabeth stood amongst the crowd of people on the deck of the ship and stared over the railing at the beautiful shores of Virginia. Off in the distance, she could see the tops of trees, as green as any back home in Wales.

"We are here, Dearie! Virginia. At last."

"It's such a beautiful place," Mary Elizabeth said as she looked about. "Every bit as pretty as Wales."

"Did my daughter think I would bring her to an ugly place?" Tad appeared at her side with a grin on his face. "Now, why, I ask ye, would I do a thing like that? Bring ye to an ugly place, indeed!"

Mam leaned over the railing, admiring the view. "The harbor is beautiful. And so are the trees. Virginia is a place of great beauty, and I thank ye for bringing us here."

"Are ye saying ye want to get off this ship then, Powells?" Tad asked. "Because I've wondered till now if perhaps ye didn't want to turn around and sail right back to England."

"Oh no," Liam gave his opinion. "I hope I never get on another ship again."

"Me either," Mary Elizabeth quickly agreed.

Mam nodded along with the children. "I'm weary with the sickness and the unsanitary conditions aboard the ship." She looked out toward the hillside once again. "I can't wait to take a walk amongst those magnificent trees. We will have a picnic just as soon as we are able."

"And swim!" Liam added, pointing to the shoreline.

"And pick berries?" Mary Elizabeth asked. Papa had told her many stories about all of the wonderful berries they would find in the springtime along Virginia's shore.

"Aye, and…," Tad looked at them all with a playful smile, "with my brother's help, we will build a home fit for the Powell family—a wonderful two-story home with a parlor downstairs and several bedrooms above."

"Tell us about the house again, Tad," Mary Elizabeth begged.

"Oh yes! Do tell us," Liam added.

Tad told them in great detail of the home he would build right here in Virginia on the Isle of Wight. "'Twill be a nice-sized home," he said with a smile. "Plenty big enough for our family and for others to come for a visit.

There will be a staircase in the front hallway, with three or perhaps even four bedrooms on the second floor. Downstairs, along with the parlor, we will have a drawing room…"

"Aye," Mam agreed, "for entertaining neighbors."

"The Morgans?" Mary Elizabeth asked.

"Of course," Mam smiled, "and many others, I hope." She turned to face Tad. "Will we have a spacious dining room?"

"If that's what ye would like, Mrs. Powell." He bowed at the waist, as if she were a queen.

Mam's eyes widened in excitement. "Yes, please. I'd like to fill it with all of our pretty dishes. I can't wait to use my teapot—ye know the one, with the pink rosebud on top?" A look of concern came over her face quite suddenly. "I do hope nothing was broken on the journey. I wrapped cloth around each item before placing it in the trunk but I'm a wee-bit nervous."

"I'm sure they are fine," Tad said, "but if they're not, we'll find places to shop, I assure ye. Merchants come from all over to the Chesapeake area to do their trading. I dare say we can fill a whole house with the beautiful things we will find ashore."

"Tell us more about the house, Tad," Mary Elizabeth urged.

He smiled and a dreamy look came into his eyes. "The kitchen will be separate from the house on the south side, a building with plenty of room for cooking up every good thing."

"Mmm." Mary Elizabeth's tummy grumbled. She missed Mam's cooking and could hardly wait to taste some of her favorite meals once again.

"Outside, in front of the house, we'll plant trees all in a row—making a grand entranceway. Then there's the land…" Tad's eyes began to glisten with joy as he spoke. "From what I've been told, we will own some of the best farming land in all of the area."

"More land than we had in Wales?" Liam asked.

"Far more."

"What will we do with all that land?" Mary Elizabeth asked.

Tad smiled. "We will grow acres and acres of wheat."

"Wheat." Mama looked pleased as she spoke the word.

"Aye," Tad said. "Many are planting tobacco, but I prefer a wheat crop." His eyes lit merrily as he continued on. "We will have a vegetable garden too, of course. We will grow plenty of corn, peas, carrots, and all sorts of good things."

"Corn," Mary Elizabeth said. "I've heard tell of it but never tasted it. Will we like it, Tad?"

"I've never had it myself, Dearie, but from what I've been told it is sure to become a favorite."

"Can we help with the planting, Tad?" Liam asked.

"Of course! We'll plant the wheat in the fall, but most of the vegetables will be planted in the springtime. I will hire local men to help with the crops, and we will have several indentured servants, as well."

"Indentured servants?" Mary Elizabeth's brow wrinkled a bit as she asked. She didn't like the word "servants" to be sure. "Are they…are they *slaves*, Tad?" She thought at once of those poor people in Barbados, and a little shiver ran down her spine.

"No, Dearie." He shook his head. "Indentured servants are men and women from other countries who want to come to America but cannot afford to pay their way. There are many aboard this very ship, in fact."

"There are?" She looked about with great curiosity. "What do they look like?"

Tad laughed, long and loud. "Why, just like ye and me, of course. And many are from our homeland. I can't wait for ye to meet them."

"Many are from Wales?" Liam's eyes widened.

"How wonderful!" Mary Elizabeth added.

Tad nodded. "I paid their passage aboard the ship, and will give them room and board on our land. In exchange, they will agree to work for me for a certain period of time. After that, I will give each person his own plot of land to farm."

"Ah, I see," Liam said with a nod.

Tad smiled. "We cannot manage this task alone. We will need a lot of help to make this patch of land a success."

"It will be a success," Mary Elizabeth said with a smile. "I know it will."

"Was it worth such a long trip to get here, then?" he quizzed.

Liam nodded. "Aye, but I'll be so happy to get off this ship once and for all."

"Me too," agreed Mary Elizabeth.

"Aye," Mam added, "but just think of the stories ye will have to tell your children and grandchildren. When they ask about your travels to America, what fun to tell of the many adventures!"

"We will, indeed," Tad added. "I, for one, would like to tell all of the Powells how very proud I am of them. It's been a hard journey, I know, and ye've been sickly at times, to be sure. But overall we've had a blessed trip. God has been with us, and He will be with us as we settle into our new home."

"Aye, 'tis true." Mam leaned over and gave him a little kiss on the cheek.

"See?" Tad said. "I said it before and I'll say it again. The Powells know how to persevere through thick and thin."

"The Morgans are known for their perseverance as well!" Mr. Morgan's voice rang out from behind them.

"I've no doubt about that!" Tad agreed.

Mary Elizabeth looked over at Abby, with a smile. "I hope to see you soon," she said with a pout.

"Oh my, yes!" Abby exclaimed. "Why, we're practically going to be neighbors. Our property is just a few miles south of yours, from what Father has told me. Mother says we'll do barn-raisings together, and help harvest crops. Why, I'm sure we'll see each other quite often."

Mary Elizabeth looked at her new friend with relief. "I'm so glad. I would miss ye terribly." Even as she spoke the words, an ache filled her heart. She missed Alva so much. Would she ever see her again?

"I want to learn how to cook that mutton dish ye've been talking so much about," Mam said to Mrs. Morgan.

"Yes, and I want your recipe for lamb stew," Mrs. Morgan echoed.

"So it's settled then," Tad said. "We'll be neighbors and friends in this new land, and from what I've been told, most everyone here is friendly."

"We'll also be free to worship as we please." Mrs. Morgan's eyes filled with tears as she spoke. "That's the most important thing of all."

"Oh yes," Mr. Morgan agreed. "No one can stop us from praising the Lord in this new land."

"In fact," Tad said, "we can start right this very minute."

"Before we get off the ship?" Liam asked.

"Aye, son." Tad took them by the hand and they gathered in a circle to pray. He thanked the Lord for giving them safe travels to the new world. He asked for the Lord's favor over the coming year. And he asked the Lord to bless each person who had traveled aboard the *Assurance* as they headed off to their new homes.

As the captain called out, "All ashore that's going ashore," Mary Elizabeth heard a familiar sound from above. She looked up to find one of the sailors overhead, letting down the sails. His singsongy voice rang out above the crowd:

I sleep beneath the hollow trees, and there I pay no rent.
Providence provides for me, and I am well content.
And a-beggin' I will go, and a-beggin' I will go,
And a-beggin' I will go, and a-beggin' I will go.

He tipped his cap at Mary Elizabeth as she followed her parents down the gangplank.

"Have a wonderful time in your new home, Miss!"

She waved back, and then turned her attentions to her family once again. With great excitement, she stepped off the ship and onto the beautiful, rich soil of Virginia.

Her father reached to sweep her into his arms, spinning her round and round.

"Welcome to America, Mary Elizabeth!" he exclaimed. "Welcome to your new home!"

Home. She thought about that word for a moment. Virginia was her home now, and she loved it more with each passing minute.

THE ISLE OF WIGHT

FTER GETTING OFF THE SHIP AT THE Isle of Wight, the family walked quite a distance into town, where they spent the night in a rented room above the local tavern. Mary Elizabeth could hardly sleep; she was so excited. She loved everything about Virginia so far—the sights, the sounds, the smells, even the language of the colonists as they scurried to and fro in the street. She especially loved the breakfast foods the family ate at the tavern the following morning.

After breakfast Tad hired a driver—a fellow by the name of Mr. Anderson—to take the family by buggy to their property.

"'Twill cost a pretty penny," he told Mam, "but there's no other way around it, short of walking. And besides, the piece of land we'll be living on is many a mile from here." Because the family's trunks and furniture would not fit in the buggy, Tad paid extra for a wagon that would follow along behind them.

As they prepared to load their things on the wagon, Tad introduced the family to Steffan and Gwyn Ludwig. "These lovely folks will be working alongside us on our land," Tad said, "and others will arrive over the next few weeks."

Mary Elizabeth smiled shyly at Gwyn, who looked to be about seventeen or so. She was a pretty girl with a splash of freckles on her nose, and she had wavy hair.

"Happy to make your acquaintance," Gwyn said, reaching out her hand for a shake.

Mary Elizabeth shook it with a smile. How wonderful to hear Gwyn's voice. "I can tell you're from Wales," she said with a giggle. "How wonderful it will be to have a new friend from our homeland."

"Wonderful for us both," Gwyn said. She then turned her attentions to the young man on her left. He looked to be no older than twenty. His golden hair glistened in the sunlight, and his eyes beamed as he looked at Gwyn. She smiled in response, and then turned to Mary Elizabeth to make introductions. "Ye've met my husband, Steffan."

"Husband?" Why, Mary Elizabeth could scarcely believe it. She hadn't realized that Gwyn was a married lady.

"The Ludwig's will be with us for a year," Tad explained. "Then they will be our neighbors. They will help us with our land, and then we will help them with theirs."

"A fair trade, to be sure," Steffan said with a lopsided grin. "And I can never thank ye enough, Mr. Powell."

"Well, think nothing of it." Tad smiled and turned to greet the fellow he'd hired to cart the family's belongings.

Mr. Anderson, the driver, was a nice man with a broad smile and a thick brown moustache that jiggled up and down when he laughed, which he did a lot, especially when he stroked the manes of his horses, Grey and Bonner. They responded to his touch with loud whinnies and even a little foot stomping. Mary Elizabeth wanted to reach out and touch them, but didn't dare. They weren't her horses, after all.

Mr. Anderson's blue eyes sparkled merrily in the afternoon sunlight, and as he reached out a hand to help Mary Elizabeth into the buggy, he gave her a little wink. "Good day, Miss."

"Good day, Sir." She nodded his direction and climbed aboard with the rest of her family. Tad sat up front with the friendly driver, but Mary Elizabeth could hear them talking, even from where she sat.

Mr. Anderson asked Tad a lot of questions. "How was your journey aboard the *Assurance*, Mr. Powell?"

"Tiring, but nice. Once the seasickness passed, that is."

Mr. Anderson chuckled. "My entire family suffered with seasickness when we made the journey years ago. Especially my youngest, Emma."

"Emma." Mary Elizabeth whispered the name. Perhaps they would be friends.

"We are a mite travel-weary," Tad said. "Happy to have our feet on dry land, to be sure."

With a smile, Mr. Anderson said, "Where are you from, Sir?"

"Wales, Sir. From the town of Laugharne. Perhaps ye've heard of Laugharne Castle."

Mr. Anderson stroked his beard thoughtfully before answering. "I do believe I read about it, back in my days as a school boy."

"Ah, 'tis a lovely place." Tad looked around at the beautiful rolling hills of Virginia before adding, "nearly as lovely as this. And we've a beautiful shoreline along the Carmathen Bay."

"I dare say, you'll find the shores of Virginia to be just as wonderful." Mr. Anderson's eyes lit with excitement as he spoke. "And the trees are unlike anything you've ever seen. Why, we've more varieties of vegetation than any place I've ever known, and wildlife in abundance."

"Sounds as if ye know the territory well," Tad said.

"Yes. I settled here with my family nearly five years ago. Came from England."

"'Twas easy to guess that," Tad said with a nod. "Though your accent isn't as strong as many to be heard aboard the ship."

"You will find that your speech changes a bit the longer you live here," Mr. Anderson said with a smile. "Before you know it, all Virginians will sound alike."

"'Tis doubtful," Mam whispered to the children with a wink.

Mary Elizabeth knew that Mam was very proud of their Welsh heritage and would work hard to preserve both their language and their customs.

"Will you be settling in the Isle of Wight?" their driver asked. "It's also known as Warrosquyoake. I do believe it's one of the nicest areas in all of Virginia."

Tad nodded. "We will, indeed. My brother arrived several months ago, and has already acquired a piece of property just south of the James River. If what he says is true, 'tis the prettiest piece of land to be had." Tad grinned from ear to ear.

"Oh, you're building a home, are you?" Mr. Anderson asked. "Have you a place to stay in the meantime?"

"My brother has built a lean-to, just big enough for the family," Tad explained. "We will stay there together until the home is completed."

"Will you be needing to hire workers, then?"

"Aye. I've another half dozen or so men coming in the next weeks, but that won't be enough. I'll speak with my brother, but I've no doubt we'll need a handful of men. My brother has drawn the plans for the house and arranged for what supplies he could in town. He has also been cutting, hewing, and drying the timber. We will want to begin building right away, while summer is still upon us."

Mr. Anderson stroked his beard once more. "Virginia is rustic, especially in comparison to the British Empire, to be sure. Supplies are hard to come by, but we manage. I've no doubt you will do the same." He brought the buggy to a halt as a wide river came into view.

"Oh, Mam, look!" Mary Elizabeth looked out of the buggy in awe. "'Tis the prettiest thing I've ever seen in all my life."

"You're looking at the James River," Mr. Anderson explained, "and I dare say you're right. It's quite a sight, isn't it?"

"Indeed," Mam said, looking at the water as it rushed across the rocks. With her hand over her heart she let out a sigh, "'Tis lovely."

"Come on out for a spell, then," Mr. Anderson said. "We'll stretch our legs a bit and get a drink before heading on. The waters of the James are cold and refreshing."

Mary Elizabeth was the first out of the buggy. She looked around, speechless. Virginia was every bit as nice as Wales. Every bit. Mam followed behind her with a smile on her face, and then came Liam. As soon as his feet hit the ground, he began to run in the direction of the river.

"Be careful, Son," Mam said. "Don't fall in."

Mr. Anderson chuckled. "If he did, we'd just fetch him out. Many a child swims in that river in the summertime, Mrs. Powell."

"Still, I don't know that Liam is a strong swimmer just yet," she explained. "So let's keep a close eye on him."

Mary Elizabeth swatted away a bumblebee. "Tad, is it always this warm in Virginia?"

"No, Darling," he said. "Only in the later summertime. 'Tis August, ye know."

"Once winter sets in…" Mr. Anderson gave a little shiver, "you will be wearing your wool coat and scarf, to be sure! Just like back home in Wales, I'd guess."

"Ooo." Mary Elizabeth gave a little shiver, just thinking about it. "I hope it's not *that* cold." She stood at the river's edge and looked out at the rolling hills and tall green trees. She breathed in a long, deep breath, noticing the lovely scent of nearby flowers. "I feel right at home here," she whispered.

"So do I," Gwyn said, drawing close with Steffan at her side. They all stared at the waters of the James River in awe.

"'Tis quite a sight," Gwyn said.

"A wonderful place to start a new life," Steffan agreed, "and a new family."

Gwyn blushed, and gave him a little punch on the arm. "'Twill be plenty of time for children after we get settled into our own place. Everything in its season, my Mam always says." At the mention of her Mam, Gwyn's eyes filled with tears. She quickly brushed them away and turned her sights to the river once more.

Mary Elizabeth couldn't imagine what it must feel like to come halfway across the world without your parents. How would Gwyn manage?

Just then, Steffan reached over and placed a little kiss on Gwyn's forehead. Mary Elizabeth watched it all with a smile.

Mam sniffed the fresh air. "It smells heavenly." She turned to face Mr. Anderson as she asked, "What is that scent?"

"Partridge berry," he explained. "Blooms every summer. Smells like fresh-cut hay, doesn't it."

"Indeed," Tad said.

"Can I pick these partridge berries and eat them?" Mary Elizabeth asked.

"No child," Tad said, "these berries aren't for eating like blackberries or raspberries, but I hear the Indians pick them and brew the leaves to make tea."

"Yes," Mr. Anderson agreed with a nod. "They use it like a medicine."

At the word "Indians," Mam looked up in alarm. They had all heard many a story about wild Indians, even before boarding the *Assurance*.

"Don't worry, Mrs. Powell," Mr. Anderson said. "There hasn't been an Indian uprising in this part of Virginia for many years."

"Still," she whispered, "it does make me a wee-bit nervous."

Tad reached over to pat her on the hand. "God has brought us all the way to this fine land, Darling, and He will protect us as we build our home."

"He will, indeed," Mam said, leaning against Tad's arm with a look of contentment on her face.

Mary Elizabeth heard one of the horses let out a whinny, and she decided it was all right to walk over and stroke their manes. As she ran her hands across Bonner's long red mane, he nuzzled his head against her hand.

"You're a natural with animals, Miss," Mr. Anderson said.

"Am I?" Mary Elizabeth gave a little shrug and reached to stroke Grey's head. He, too, nuzzled against her hand and let out a contented "nay" sound. Everyone laughed.

"Looks like I'll have to put you in charge of our horses, Mary Elizabeth," Tad said, as he approached from behind.

She couldn't tell if he was teasing or not, but hoped he wasn't. "Oh Tad! I would love that. I really, really would."

She leaned against Grey and looked out over the green leaves on the trees and the many wildflowers. She breathed in the fresh scent of the partridge berries and wondered what it would be like to actually meet a real Indian. As she pondered all of these things, she found herself looking at the clear, rippling waters of the James River. Perhaps one day she and Liam would get to swim in that river like she did in the bay at home.

Home. She thought about that word for a moment. Virginia was her home now, and she loved it more with each passing minute.

A short while later, Mr. Anderson urged everyone to climb aboard the buggy once again. "We will be at your property in less than half an hour," he explained.

True to his word, they arrived at Uncle Gaynor's lean-to a short while later. Mary Elizabeth noticed her Uncle's beard had grown even longer since she had seen him last, and his skin was tanned and healthy-looking.

He met them with a loud shout. "Brother!"

"Brother!" Tad replied, climbing down from the buggy and giving his younger brother a warm hug.

"I was starting to think I would never see you." Uncle Gaynor patted Tad on the back.

"Aye. 'Twas a long trip," Tad explained, "but we are here now, and anxious to be building."

"Come first and see your land." A smile as broad as the James River crossed Uncle Gaynor's face.

The whole family, along with Mr. Anderson and the Ludwigs, walked the land for hours, looking at the trees, the wide rolling hills, and the shoreline of the James River.

"Gaynor, you've selected a prime piece of land," Tad said when they were done, "and I can hardly wait to build a house here."

"Aye," Mam agreed. "How wonderful it will be to have a home once again."

"Oh yes," Mary Elizabeth echoed. "How wonderful to have our very own home."

In that happy frame of mind, the Powell family spent the very first night on their very own piece of land in the breathtaking new place called Virginia.

"Indeed!" Tad hollered down from the rooftop. "A very big house for a very big family!"

A Big House

MARY ELIZABETH CLUTCHED HER RAG doll in her arms and gazed up at the men working on their house. Already they had put up the large outside walls. Now Tad and the others were hard at work on the rooftop.

"Tad, our house is so big!" She shouted to be heard above all the noise.

"Indeed!" Tad hollered down from the rooftop. "A very big house for a very big family!"

Very big family? Mary Elizabeth wondered about that. Big? Why, it was just Mam, Tad, Liam, and herself. And Uncle Gaynor, of course. He would stay with them until his own home could be built. The Ludwig's would stay on in the lean-to until a proper home could be built for them.

Mam appeared at her side and rested a hand upon her shoulder. "'Twill be a much larger house than the one in Wales, to be sure."

"Aye, but I don't understand," Mary Elizabeth said, looking at her Mam curiously. "Tad said we had a very *big* family. What did he mean?"

Mam placed a hand on her belly and flashed a suspicious smile.

"Oh, Mam!" Mary Elizabeth exclaimed. "Are ye having a baby? Am I going to have a wee baby brother or sister?"

"Aye," Mam answered with a smile. "I've wanted to tell ye for weeks, ever since we arrived, but Tad was hoping we could wait to surprise ye children when the house was complete." Mam looked up at the rooftop where Tad continued to work. "Looks like he gave away our little surprise."

Mary Elizabeth clapped her hands in glee. "When will the baby be born, Mam?"

"'Twill be a springtime lad or lassie," Mam said. "The wee one will arrive in late April, most likely."

Mary Elizabeth leaned against Mam and gave her a warm hug. "Oh, I can't wait to meet her!"

"Her?" Mam grinned. "What makes ye so sure ye'll be having a sister, then?"

A giggle escaped from Mary Elizabeth's lips. "I don't know. I just hope it's a girl. I already have a brother, after all."

"Brothers are a very good thing to have," Mam said. "Look at Liam. He's such a hard worker."

Sure enough, Liam, small as he was, worked hard alongside the men. Still, Elizabeth couldn't help but think a little sister would be a nice thing to have too.

"When will the house be finished?" She asked, as she and Mam gazed upward at Tad. "The babe will be needing a nursery."

"'Tis a question for your father, but I've a mind to think we'll be in the new house before winter. Most of the woodwork for the outside has been done, and that's the hardest part. The men will finish the roof and begin the work on the inside, putting up walls and a lovely staircase."

Mary Elizabeth looked out at all the new men who now worked with Tad. What was it Tad had called them? Indentured servants? They didn't look like servants a'tall. Why, they just looked like friends and family as they worked together alongside her father.

"It's nearly October already," Mary Elizabeth said. "I can scarcely believe we've been here six weeks, can you?" Even as she spoke the words, she felt an ache in her heart for her dear friend Alva, back at home in Wales. She hugged her doll a bit tighter, thinking of her.

Mam rubbed her back. "I'm tired of sleeping in the lean-to, all of us pressed together in such a small place. I can hardly wait to sleep in my own bed. Your Tad has promised a mattress made of the softest corn shucks. Should be a mite more comfortable than the straw mat we've been sharing." She smiled. "But your Tad always says the Powells have a strong constitution."

"What does that mean?" Mary Elizabeth asked. "A strong con..sti…" She couldn't pronounce the word, so she stopped in the middle of it.

"Constitution," Mam repeated. "It means the Powells *persevere* till the very end. Do ye know what that means—persevere?"

Mary Elizabeth shrugged. "I've heard Tad tell of it."

"It means we finish what we've started, even when the task is very, very difficult."

"Oh. I understand." Mary Elizabeth nodded. Surely Tad had the strongest constitution of all, for he persevered through every trial. Just last week, he had injured his hand working. Had he stopped? No, he had continued on. And just a few days later when all the other men stopped working because of the rain, Tad continued on, working by himself. Yes, he surely knew what it meant to persevere.

From now on, Mary Elizabeth decided, she would prove that she could persevere too. She would not complain while helping Mam prepare food for the men. She wouldn't fuss about having to keep an eye on Liam when the others were too busy. She would persevere, just like Tad.

Her thoughts shifted again to the new house. How wonderful it would be to sleep in a bed—a real bed—again. "I can't wait!" she exclaimed.

Just then, Tad let out a laugh, long and loud. He almost lost his grip on the rooftop in the process.

Mam put her hand to her heart. "Your Tad has a fine sense of humor, to be sure. But he'll be tumbling from the rooftop if he doesn't pay attention to what he's doing!"

Mary Elizabeth giggled. She knew Tad would be safe. And she loved his funny sense of humor. In fact, she wanted to be just like him when she grew up. Already folks said she looked like him—the same brown wavy hair, the same blue eyes, the same splattering of freckles on her arms and face. Yes, she hoped to be like Tad in most every way, but especially when it came to his sense of humor.

"Are ye ready for some food, Daughter?" Mam asked. "'Tis almost time to feed the men their noon meal."

"Aye." Mary Elizabeth followed her Mam to the stone building, just a few yards away, that Tad and the others had built last week. The new structure served as a kitchen. It had a great fireplace, a large oven made of brick, and plenty of room to store their pans, which had arrived safely from Wales in one of the large trunks.

Gwyn stirred the stew in a large pot. Mam joined her, lifting the ladle to have a little taste of the rabbit stew.

"I believe this stew will stick to the ribs of the workers and give them the energy to work all afternoon," Mam said with a smile.

The wonderful aroma of freshly baked bread filled the place, and Mary Elizabeth sniffed the air, wishing she could have a piece right here and now. Instead, she focused her attentions on the work at hand. She filled large crock bowls full of the steamy hot stew, and then went outside to ring the large bell. The men, upon hearing the sound, began to call out: "Mealtime!"

Soon everyone was seated all around—some on tree stumps, others on the ground, eating the stew and home-made bread.

"I dare say, this is the best food I've had in a month of Sundays," Steffan said.

"You say that every time," Mary Elizabeth giggled.

"Do I, now?" He gave a little wink, and then finished up his meal. He stood and rubbed his belly. "A man could work all day long after tasting Gwyn's cooking."

Gwyn's cheeks flamed bright red, and she shooed her husband away.

"Indeed," the other men agreed.

And that's just what they did. Tad and the other men worked all day long. And they worked the day after and the day after that. In fact, they worked well into the fall, when the leaves turned to bright red and the water in the James River ran colder than ever.

All the while, Mary Elizabeth looked on with great joy as the house began to look more like a home. She especially loved the look of the roof, which was steep, unlike the one back home in Wales. And she enjoyed gazing up at the towering chimney, which was made of bricks. There were shutters on the windows, which Uncle Gaynor had crafted. Inside, the house had raised floors, and three large rooms—a parlor, a drawing room, and a dining hall.

Upstairs was her favorite part, however. There were four spacious bedrooms with a long hallway separating them. She could hardly wait to see the house completed.

The men continued to work, day after day, as the last of the autumn leaves tumbled from the trees. They worked from early in the morning until late at night when the crisp cold October winds turned chilly. Each day, Mary Elizabeth helped Mam and Gwyn prepare food for the workers. Each day she grew to love her new friends and neighbors more. She especially loved getting to know Gwyn. Truly, they were like sisters in no time a'tall.

In late October the Morgan family came for a visit and stayed all day so that Mr. Morgan could help Tad with the inside of the house. Many of the pieces of furniture had been brought over on the ship and brought to the house on the large wagon—the china cabinet, for example, and Mam's harpsichord. The other pieces—like the beds and the dining room table, had to be crafted from wood. Mr.

Morgan was a fine craftsman, and spent many hours on the design of the table and several chairs.

Mary Elizabeth was thrilled to see Abby and her older sister, Hope. Mary Elizabeth couldn't help but notice that Uncle Gaynor often gave Hope a shy smile, which she usually returned with a blush in her cheeks.

Abby and Mary Elizabeth spent most of the day helping their mothers prepare meals for the men. They took turns looking after the hog that was roasting on the spit, but they had a chance to sneak off to the edge of the river for a quiet conversation in the late afternoon.

"Do you love Virginia as much as I do?" Abby asked, leaning against a large oak tree.

"Oh yes," Mary Elizabeth agreed. "It's wonderful here, but it's getting colder every day."

"True. Mother says fall will be over before we know it," Abby said.

"We should enjoy it while we can," Mary Elizabeth replied.

The two had a wonderful time talking and playing, but before they knew it, they had to part ways.

"We really must be on our way before it gets dark," Mrs. Morgan explained. The clip-clop of horse's hooves made a merry sound as they traveled down the road, away from the Powell's home. Mary Elizabeth was awfully sad to see her friend leave, but Tad's announcement gave her reason to celebrate.

"Powell family!" he exclaimed with a happy smile, "Ye may enter your new home. At last!"

"Dear Lord," he prayed, "we bless Thee for this, Thy bounty. Thank Ye for bringing us to this fine land, and for all of Thy many blessings. Amen."

SETTLING IN

HE FIRST DAYS IN THE BIG HOUSE WERE filled with activity. Mam loved seeing her furniture inside, especially the table and chairs Tad and Mr. Morgan had made.

"I don't believe I've ever seen anything finer!" she exclaimed.

By the third day, the furniture was in place and the mattresses on the beds were stuffed with soft corn shucks. Tad and Liam headed out to the fields early in the morning, and Mam went to work emptying the family's trunks so that she could begin the task of decorating with her pretty things from Wales. This was her favorite part of all. Mary Elizabeth could tell from the look of joy on her face.

Gwyn helped Mam unpack. Her eyes grew large as she saw the beautiful things for the first time. "Oh, Mrs. Powell!" She put a hand to her heart as she spoke. "It's so fine!" Mam just smiled as they unloaded vases and clocks, figurines, and candlesticks. Best of all, they found Mam's beautiful china teapot—still perfect in every way.

"Lord be praised!" Mam grabbed it and hugged it tight. "I can't believe it. Not a break in it."

She turned to give Gwyn a smile. "This little teapot makes the finest tea in all the world," she said, "and I will get right to work brewing some!"

True to her word, she brewed up a pot of tea right away. Mary Elizabeth thought it was the finest she had ever tasted, and Gwyn agreed.

After their tea break, everything had to be dusted. Gwyn worked hard to make sure the Powell's things looked lovely. All the while, she sang a little Welsh song to Mary Elizabeth. A faraway look came into her eyes as she sang, but she never stopped working.

"Your singing is so pretty, Gwyn," Mary Elizabeth said when she finally stopped, "and I've missed hearing that song, to be sure."

"Reminds me of home," Gwyn explained with a little wink.

Mam came into the room at that very moment and made an announcement. "I do believe it's time to share some of my favorite recipes with Gwyn," she exclaimed.

"Oh, thank ye, Mrs. Powell," Gwyn said with excitement. "I long to cook as well as ye do."

"How wonderful!" Mary Elizabeth clapped her hands. "I miss our food from Wales!" She traipsed along behind

Mam and Gwyn out to the separate kitchen, where Mam spent nearly an hour explaining how to make some of their Welsh favorites. She told Gwyn all about Welsh Rarebit, cheese on toast, and then she explained how to make one of Mary Elizabeth's very favorite things: Bara Brith.

"Bara Brith!" Gwyn grew more excited. "Why, my own Mam made Bara Brith all the time." A homesick look came in her eyes at once.

"Not as good as Mam's, I'm sure!" Mary Elizabeth said, before clamping her hand over her mouth in embarrassment. "'Tis the tastiest speckled bread ye've ever tasted!"

Gwyn giggled and paid close attention as Mam gave cooking instructions.

"The speckles are dried fruit or dates," Mam said. "Bara Brith is a Powell favorite!"

"And mine as well," Gwyn agreed.

Together, the ladies shared a wonderful time in the kitchen, mixing up bread dough and baking till the whole room grew warm from the oven.

After the cooking lesson, Mam went back to the main house to lie down on her new bed to rest. Mary Elizabeth knew that Mam would need much rest over the coming months, and she wanted to help in any way she could.

While Mam slept, Mary Elizabeth went outside to search for Tad. She found him with Uncle Gaynor and Steffan and several other men out in the fields. They were using a large plow to till the ground. Mary Elizabeth watched from a distance, longing to run her fingers through the plow horse's long dark manes.

Finally, when the men took a break, she drew closer. "What are ye doing, Tad?" she asked, pulling her shawl tight around her shoulders.

He looked up and wiped his brow with the back of his hand. "Preparing the ground to plant the wheat."

"Aren't ye cold?"

"No, Darlin'," he explained. "Hard work keeps me warm, and we must move quickly." He looked over at Steffan with a nod. "'Tis mighty late in the season to plant, but Mr. Anderson says we have just enough time, if we hurry." Tad looked out over the fields and then turned back to Mary Elizabeth, his expression more serious. "If we don't plant in the fall, there will be no harvest in the summer."

Steffan nodded and smiled broadly. "You will have your harvest, Mister Powell," he said. "You will. Remember that story in the Bible about having faith as tiny as a mustard seed?"

"Indeed," Tad said, "and if there's anything I've come to appreciate, it's a story about seed planting!"

Tad, Uncle Gaynor, Steffan, and many other men plowed and prepared the land. Mary Elizabeth offered to help, and Tad allowed her to follow along behind the men and rake the ground. She worked until her hands were blistered and raw.

"Have ye had enough fun yet, Daughter?" Tad asked, finally. "Perhaps ye would prefer to help your Mam in the house?"

"Aye," Mary Elizabeth agreed. "I would enjoy being indoors." She unwrapped the dirty strips of cloth from her red, sore hands and held them up for him to look at. "My hands are weary from the work."

Tad nodded with an understanding smile and held his up too.

"Oh, Tad!" Mary Elizabeth exclaimed. "How will ye keep working with your hands in such a state?"

He wrapped strips of cloth around his hands and shrugged. "Don't ye be worrying about your Tad," he explained. "Remember what I told ye. We Powells always persevere."

She couldn't help but smile. "I remember, Tad." She knew her father would work hard, no matter the cost. That's what the Powells did. They persevered.

"Speaking of perseverance," Tad said, "I have some news for ye."

"News?"

"Aye." He gave her a little wink. "I've no doubt ye've been missing your lessons."

Mary Elizabeth shook her head. "I don't miss them, Tad. Not a'tall."

"Ah. I guessed as much."

"There's been no time for lessons. Not with so much work to be done."

"True," he said, "but winter will be upon us before we know it, and the days will slow down. I've hired a tutor to work with ye children."

"A tutor?"

"Aye," he chuckled, "but don't be nervous, child. She won't work ye too hard."

"Why can't Gwyn tutor us?" Mary Elizabeth asked.

"She is far too busy helping Mam," he explained. "I have someone else in mind."

"Who, Tad? Who?" She asked, bouncing up and down in excitement.

"Mr. Morgan's daughter, Hope, will stay with us three days a week while the weather is good. She will teach Liam to read and help ye with your lessons—spelling, arithmetic, and penmanship. She will also tutor ye in music and help ye with your needlework. Ye know your Mam has been wanting ye to work on your sampler."

"But, Tad…" Mary Elizabeth didn't want to worry about lessons, not with so many things going on.

"Now child…" he said.

She sighed. Perhaps it would be fun to have Hope over. Besides, Uncle Gaynor seemed to love it when Hope came to visit. He got all nervous and fumbling-like, and stammered when he spoke. It seemed he could hardly take his eyes off her. And she seemed to enjoy his attention, as well, blushing whenever he took her arm to help her across a mud puddle or a hole in the road.

Yes, Hope would do just fine.

After talking with Tad, Mary Elizabeth went back into the house to see if Mam needed her help preparing dinner. By the time Tad came into the house from the fields, the dinner table was filled with several of his favorite foods. The entire Powell family settled down for their first real Welsh meal since arriving in America. Tad looked as happy as could be as he folded his hands to lead the family in prayer.

"Dear Lord," he prayed, "we bless Thee for this, thy bounty. Thank Ye for bringing us to this fine land, and for all of Your many blessings. Amen."

"Amen," everyone echoed.

Mary Elizabeth looked across the table with a smile on her face. She couldn't wait to taste Mam's good food, but more than that, she couldn't wait to see what amazing things the next few weeks and months would hold in her wonderful new home called Virginia.

"That boy was made for farm life," Tad often said.

LIFE ON THE FARM

AN EARLY WINTER CHILL SEEMED TO come on suddenly, just after Tad and the other men got the wheat planted. The winds blew cold across the fields, starting in mid-November.

Tad now spent his days tending to the livestock, making sure the mules and horses were fed each morning. With the help of the other men, he butchered meat—hogs, cows, deer, and even rabbits—so the family would have plenty to eat over the coming months. The farm grew daily, as more men came to work for Tad, some arriving from faraway places.

Steffan and one of the other men, a fellow named Micah, taught Liam how to milk the cows. He quickly grew to love this task. He even seemed to enjoy fetching eggs from the henhouse and caring for the hunting dogs.

"That boy was made for farm life," Tad often said.

Mary Elizabeth helped Mam and Gwyn around the house, grinding corn, churning butter, even spinning and weaving cloth. She carried armloads of vegetables, which they had acquired from Mr. Anderson, into the root cellar. Next spring they would grow their own vegetables. Tad said so. They would plant as soon as the first wildflowers grew.

Mary Elizabeth didn't mind the hard work. She had a lot of fun learning things like candle-making and making cheese. Still, there was one task above all that she dreaded: killing chickens.

"Mam, do we have to?" she asked one chilly November morning.

"Ye love it when Gwyn roasts chicken, don't ye, Dearie?" Mam asked. "In fact, I seem to remember hearing ye say roast chicken was one of your very favorite meals."

"Yes, but…"

"No buts, Mary Elizabeth. 'Tis a task that must be done."

So she worked alongside Mam and Gwyn, closing her eyes as they broke the necks of the chickens, and then helping pluck the feathers after the birds had been dipped in scalding water. She would sooner have done almost anything—even lessons—but she knew Mam was right. She must persevere no matter what. Tad would want her to.

Hope arrived at their house each Tuesday and stayed until Friday. Uncle Gaynor was happy to escort her when the weather was poor, and from the flush in Hope's cheeks, Mary Elizabeth could tell she was happy to receive his help. Hope taught the children many lessons—everything from the King's English to excellent penmanship. Mary Elizabeth grew to love her like an older sister, and what fun to watch Hope and Gwyn become "forever friends" as well.

One Tuesday in late November, the weather was too bad for Hope to come.

"Will it snow, Tad?" Mary Elizabeth asked one morning as she peered out of the window.

"'Tis possible we could see snow before Christmas, Dearie," he said.

A little shiver ran down Mary Elizabeth's spine. "I rather hoped it would be warm in Virginia," she said with a sigh.

Tad laughed. "Darling, the winter's are more mild here than in Wales, to be sure. But when it does snow ye will love it. You and Liam can go sledding on the hillside and build snowmen. And besides…" he said, leaning in close to give her a kiss on the cheek, "a white Christmas is a wonderful thing, indeed."

"Oh, Christmas!" In the rush to get the house built and the land plowed, Mary Elizabeth had almost forgotten about her favorite holiday.

She followed along behind Tad as he went into the drawing room to light a fire in the fireplace. As the flames danced red and orange, she settled onto a chair to ask Tad some questions that had been on her mind for weeks now.

"Tad, will I ever see Alva again?" Mary Elizabeth bit her lip and tried to keep the tears from flowing.

Her father took a seat nearby before answering. "Are ye missing your friend, Daughter?"

"Aye." She brushed away a loose tear and focused on his eyes as he answered.

"There are a great many fine people I'm missing, as well," he said. "My brothers and sisters."

"At least Uncle Gaynor is here."

"Yes, Lord be praised. But I've left behind many a friend and family member in Wales, to be sure." His face grew more serious as he spoke. "Mary Elizabeth, I feel you're old enough to understand grown-up things. May I speak frankly with ye?"

"Of course, Tad." She sat up tall in the chair, proud of the fact that her father thought her old enough to talk to about grown-up things.

"Times were hard back home, Daughter. Conditions were poor and wages too low. We were blessed, in that we had property to sell, but many were not so fortunate. They came to the New World with little but the clothes on their backs."

"Like some of the men you've hired?" she asked.

"Aye," he nodded, "and I want to care for them and make sure they have good lives. I also want them to know that they can worship God freely here in Virginia. Ye'll notice I read from my Bible quite often."

"Yes, Tad."

"Here in Virginia we are free to worship as we please. No one tells us what we must believe. We read this Bible—God's Holy Word—and decide for ourselves. Do ye understand?"

"Yes, Tad."

"We must thank God every day for this freedom," he explained. "And we must read the Word of God continually, so that we can come to know the Lord more and more with each passing day. The Bible says that we are to study to show ourselves approved…"

"Study, like I study my lessons?" she asked.

"Aye, that's it." He grinned and opened the Bible. "Now, go and fetch your brother. Just because Miss Hope can't be here today doesn't mean we won't have lessons."

Mary Elizabeth ran off to find Liam. Then, together, they sat at Tad's feet and listened to him read from the big black family Bible.

"The baby is here!" Mary Elizabeth
jumped up and down in delight.

Nine

NEW LIFE

CHRISTMAS CAME AND WENT. WINTER passed slowly, but the warm days of spring came at last. Mary Elizabeth looked forward to romping and playing in the fields after her lessons and chores each day. The beautiful spring flowers outside the window proved to be much of a distraction for Mary Elizabeth.

"Oh, Hope, look!" she said, one fine day while peering out the window.

"What is it, Mary Elizabeth?"

Mary Elizabeth turned toward Hope, clapping her hands in glee. "Just look at all of the beautiful flowers." The wildflowers bloomed in the fields. There were violets as blue as the skies above, and dozens of black-eyed Susans, with their bright yellow leaves. There were gold dandelions, which always made Liam sneeze, and wild geraniums, with petals as soft and pink as silk. Best of all, she loved the buttercups, for they bloomed in both yellow and pink.

"Virginia is lovely in April," Hope said as she joined her at the window. "The flowers remind me of the countryside near our home in England."

"They remind me of the meadow near Laugharne Castle," Mam said as she entered the room.

"Yes, that's right. I remember," Mary Elizabeth said, surprised as she realized she hadn't missed Wales for some time now. "I'd almost forgotten about Laugharne Castle, Mam. Do you think I'll forget about our homeland entirely?"

"'Tis not possible, for every day I will tell a little story to remind ye. We will sing Welsh songs and eat the same foods ye've always loved. Nay, child. I won't let ye forget, I promise."

"Thank you, Mam." With a smile, Mary Elizabeth looked around to make sure her morning chores and lessons were complete before asking the question on her heart. "May I go outside to play?"

An odd look crossed Mam's face, and she ran her hand across her belly, which had grown quite large over the past few months. Any day now the baby would arrive. Mary Elizabeth could hardly wait to see if the Lord would give her a baby brother or a baby sister. Mam's forehead wrinkled and she made a funny face.

"Are you alright?" Hope asked.

"Should I call for Tad?" Mary Elizabeth offered.

"No. 'Tis probably just an upset stomach," Mam said. "Now go on and take your brother. Running in the fields will do him some good. I will ring the bell when dinner time comes."

"I will pick some flowers today," Mary Elizabeth announced as they opened the front door. "Pink butter-cups—for the table in the dining hall!" She and Liam ran from the front door into the field near the house.

"Race you to the river," Liam shouted. He took off running ahead of her, not even looking back.

"No, Liam," she called out in fear. "You know Tad said not to go near the river. You might fall in, and you're not a strong swimmer."

He pouted but obeyed, turning in the direction of the field on the east side of the house, far from the water's edge.

When they arrived in the field, the lovely aroma of the pink buttercups greeted them. Mary Elizabeth picked a fistful and held them in her hand, spinning round and round. "They're so pretty!"

"You're such a *girl!*" Liam exclaimed. "Picking flowers. Let's do something fun. Let's look for bugs or snakes." His eyes grew large. "Tad says he found a snake the other day."

"Mercy," Mary Elizabeth said, "I don't want to find snakes. And I don't like bugs, either. I just want to pick flowers for Mam and the baby."

Liam groaned. "You're no fun, Sister."

"I dare say, I'm the most fun person I know!" she responded.

They played together until the bell rang for dinner. As Mary Elizabeth approached the house, she saw that Gwyn had rung the bell instead of Mam.

"I brought flowers for Mam!" she said, holding them up for Gwyn to see. "Can we put them on the dinner table?"

"You can." Gwyn gave her a funny look, "but your Mam is very busy right now and can't be disturbed. She won't be joining ye at the dinner table."

"What?" Liam looked surprised. "Is she sick?"

Gwyn smiled. "She's hard at work, bringing a baby into this world."

"Oh, Gwyn!" Mary Elizabeth jumped up and down. "Is it time? Is Mam having the baby?"

When Gwyn nodded, Mary Elizabeth said, "I want to go to her. Please let me see her."

"Oh, I don't know, child. We've sent for Mrs. Morgan, and she will arrive soon."

"Please, Gwyn," Mary Elizabeth begged. "I'll only stay a minute, but I must see Mam. I must."

"I'll peek in her room and ask."

Moments later, Gwyn appeared with a broad smile. "Your Mam is wanting ye, child. But just for a moment or two."

Mary Elizabeth nodded and then tiptoed into her mother's room, still clutching the flowers in her hand. She found Mam in the bed, dressed in a white nightgown. Her face was red and she looked to be in terrible pain.

"Oh, Mam, are you going to be alright?"

Mam nodded, but gripped the post on the bed with her hand. "Hope has been a big help. So has Gwyn. But I do wish Mrs. Morgan would arrive soon. She will know just what to do."

"I can help," Mary Elizabeth whispered. "Tad says I'm old enough for grown-up things. What can I do?"

"Well…" Mam paused a moment, looking around the room, "we will need the cradle brought in and tidied up. And there are some blankets in the linen cupboard to go inside. Can you help me prepare a place for the baby, Daughter?"

"I can!"

"But first, eat your dinner." Mam gripped the bedpost again, a look of pain coming across her face. "I need ye to keep up your strength."

Mary Elizabeth put the buttercups in a lovely vase, determined to give them to her Mam as soon as the baby arrived. Then she ate as fast as she could. Just as she finished up, Tad appeared with Mrs. Morgan at his side. Together, they rushed to Mam's room, where Mrs. Morgan went in to attend to her.

"Will she be alright, Tad?" Mary Elizabeth asked.

"Aye." Tad smiled. "Your Mam will do just fine; now don't ye be worrying your pretty head about anything at all."

"What can I do?"

"Pray, child. Pray for a healthy baby, and for your Mam's pain to be brief."

Mary Elizabeth did just that. She went to her bedroom and knelt at the side of the bed, where she offered up a long prayer for her Mam and the baby.

When she came out of her room, she prepared the cradle and then looked for Liam. She couldn't seem to find him anywhere. She asked Gwyn, but she was busy in the kitchen. She asked Steffan, but he was busy putting shoes on one of the horses. Mary Elizabeth searched every room in the house, but couldn't find him anywhere. Finally, growing afraid, she went in search of Tad.

"I can't find Liam anywhere," she explained, her heart pounding wildly. "He wanted to look for snakes, and I'm afraid he might have gone to the river."

"The river?" Tad's eyes grew large. He went at once in search of Liam.

Some time later, just as Mrs. Morgan came out to ask about a wet cloth for Mam's forehead, Tad entered the house with Liam—his clothes soaking wet and dirty—in his arms.

"Liam, what has happened to you?" Mary Elizabeth asked.

"I… I…"

"He fell in the river," Tad explained. "Thankfully I arrived straight-away and fetched him out. Not a moment too soon."

"Tad saved my life." Liam looked up with a sheepish smile.

Their father's eyes filled with tears. "Son, I don't know what I would've done, if something had happened to ye."

A shiver ran down Mary Elizabeth's spine and she hugged her brother. What if Tad had lost one child on the very day another one entered the world? Thankfully, Liam was fine, though he had certainly disobeyed.

"I told you not to go near the river," Mary Elizabeth whispered.

Liam offered up a sheepish shrug, and whispered, "I'm sorry."

"For a father to lose his son would be a difficult thing, indeed." Tad grew silent for a moment, and then turned to the children with a serious look on his face. "'Tis time I told ye another Father and Son story—one that will change your life forever." Liam looked a bit confused, but he listened closely as Tad explained. So did Mary Elizabeth.

"The father in this story is our heavenly Father." Tad's eyes grew misty as he spoke.

"God?" Liam asked.

"Aye," Tad said, "and His Son, Jesus Christ, who came as a babe in a manger."

"I remember that story!" Liam said, his eyes lighting up. "The Christmas story!"

"Yes," Tad said. "It begins as a Christmas story, but ends as a story of sacrifice. God the Father knew that His Son would one day die on a cross."

"How sad." Liam's lips curled down in a little pout.

"'Twas sad," Tad agreed, "but it was also a happy story, for when Jesus died on the cross at Calvary, He did so for ye and me."

"You and me?" Liam looked more confused than ever. "Jesus died for me?"

"Aye," Tad nodded. "Indeed, He did. He gave His life as a sacrifice for our sins. When we ask Jesus Christ to live in our hearts, He washes away every bad thing we've ever done."

"Things like playing near the river when I wasn't supposed to?" Liam asked.

"Aye, things like that," Tad said with a smile. "And many more things. If ye ask Jesus to come and live in your heart and forgive ye of your sins, He will do it right away—and your life will never be the same!"

"I want a new life!" Liam's face lit up with great joy. "I want to be forgiven of my sins. I want to ask Jesus to live in my heart."

Mary Elizabeth's eyes filled with tears as Tad led Liam in a prayer. "Dear Jesus," Tad started, and Liam echoed, "come and live in my heart. Be my Lord and Savior.

Thank You for dying on the cross for me. Thank You for Your sacrifice. Please forgive me for my sins. Cleanse me and make me brand new. Thank You for being my Lord. In Jesus' name, amen!"

Afterwards, Liam looked up, eyes bright. "Tad, am I really brand new?"

"Ye are, Son." Tad smiled. "Ye are."

Just then, Mam let out a whimper from the bedroom, and Tad turned his attentions back to helping Mrs. Morgan prepare the cloths. Mary Elizabeth embraced Liam and then sent him off to his bedroom to change into clean, dry clothes.

Just as he reappeared in the hallway, the sound of a baby's cry echoed forth.

"The baby is here!" Mary Elizabeth jumped up and down in delight.

She waited until she could hardly wait any longer. Finally, Mrs. Morgan opened up the door and gestured for Tad to come inside. Mary Elizabeth wanted to go too, but knew she must be patient. Her time would come. She reached for the vase of pink buttercups, anxious to carry them into her Mam's room.

Moments later, Tad swung the door open and welcomed Mary Elizabeth and Liam inside. "Come on in, Powell children!" he exclaimed. "Come and meet your new baby sister!"

"Tad is good to everyone," Mary Elizabeth explained. "I know it's because he loves the Lord. It shows in everything he does."

SPRING

AM AND TAD NAMED THE NEW baby girl Virginia, after the place where she was born.

"Virginia." As the word rolled across Mary Elizabeth's lips, she loved it even more than ever.

Baby Virginia had the softest white skin Mary Elizabeth had ever seen, and cheeks as pink as the buttercups she had placed in the vase on Mam's bedside table. Mam dressed the baby in a lovely white gown, which Gwyn pulled from the trunk.

"'Twas your baby dress, Mary Elizabeth," Mam said with a smile.

"Really?" She looked at the gown more closely. "I don't remember."

"Of course not! Ye were a wee one at the time, to be sure!"

Everyone had a hearty laugh, but Mary Elizabeth was distracted by the look of wonder in Gwyn's eyes as she gazed down at the newborn.

"One day I will have a wee babe of my own," Gwyn whispered.

"Indeed, you shall!" Mam said.

"One day soon," Gwyn said. She turned to face mother with a suspicious smile.

"Girl, speak it plain," Mam said. "Are ye and Steffan expecting a wee one as well?"

"We are!" Gwyn's face lit up with joy. "We figure the babe to arrive in late fall. Perhaps we will be in our own house by then."

"We will work together to make it happen," Tad said, with a determined sound in his voice. "And congratulations to ye both! I cannot wait to see Steffan, to give him a slap on the back!"

"The babes will grow up together," Mam said, with a look of wonder in her eyes. "Surely they will be wonderful friends."

"Surely." Gwyn let out a playful giggle and rubbed her hand across her tummy.

Overcome with joy, Mary Elizabeth looked down at her little sister and felt her heart swell with pride. "Oh, Mam. She looks just like a baby doll!"

"She does, indeed," Tad agreed, "but I dare say Virginia Lee Powell is a sure sight prettier than any doll."

Mary Elizabeth had to agree. And her baby sister wasn't just pretty—she was good. She cooed and smiled much of the time, and slept a lot too. Sometimes she cried in soft whimpers, but was usually hushed right away when Mam held her close and rocked her to sleep. Mary Elizabeth loved holding her too, but Liam didn't care to.

"I'm afraid she will break," he said.

Mary Elizabeth just laughed. *Boys could be so funny sometimes,* she thought.

Shortly after the baby was born, Tad announced that the time had come to plant the spring vegetable garden. Mary Elizabeth and Liam asked if they could help.

"I suppose a day away from your lessons won't hurt ye," Tad said with a grin. "And I could use the extra hands, to be sure."

Together, they cleared the patch of land. Liam shoveled at the dirt and Mary Elizabeth plucked up weeds. Then, with Tad's help, they prepared the soil, making long mounds of dirt. Tad went along and poked holes in the dirt, ready to do the planting.

"What should we do first?" he asked.

"Potatoes!" Mary Elizabeth squealed. They were her very favorite.

"Fine." Tad picked up the sack of potato eyes and walked down a long mound of dirt, dropping them every foot or so into the holes he had prepared. Liam followed along behind him, covering over the holes with dirt.

"Peas next?" Tad asked.

"Yes, please." Mary Elizabeth helped him plant the peas and then the corn. After that, they worked hard to plant the squash and green beans. Mary Elizabeth worked until her back ached and her fingers blistered.

When they were finished, they stepped back to have a look at their work.

"How long until they grow?" Liam asked. "Can we eat the vegetables tomorrow?"

"Tomorrow?" Tad laughed. "No, Son. Not tomorrow or the day after. When we plant a new crop, we must wait until the harvest. Remember, we planted the wheat months ago, and it won't be ready till the summertime."

Liam sighed. "I don't like to wait, Tad."

"I know. I get impatient too, but remember what I always say—we Powells need to…"

"Persevere!" they all shouted together.

"Aye," Tad agreed, "and it takes great patience to persevere. Remember how patient we had to be on the ship?"

Liam groaned and made a face. "Yes. I never want to do that again."

"Me either," Mary Elizabeth agreed.

"Remember how patient we had to be when we were building the house?" Tad asked.

"Yes," both children responded.

"Think of how patient your Mam had to be during the months she was expecting baby Virginia." A smile came across Tad's face. "She surely had to persevere."

Mary Elizabeth nodded.

Tad then quoted one of his favorite Bible verses from the book of James chapter one, verse twelve. He had shared it with the children quite often, but Mary Elizabeth never grew tired of hearing it: *Blessed is the man that endureth temptation: for when he is tried, he shall receive the crown of life, which the Lord hath promised to them that love him.*

Liam tugged on Tad's sleeve. "But you didn't tell us how long we will have to wait for the vegetables."

"Ah." Tad looked over the field with a contented smile. "The squash and carrots will be ready in sixty days. Same with the green beans."

"Sixty days?" Mary Elizabeth did the math in her head. "That's two months. We can't eat the squash or carrots for two months?"

"No." Tad shook his head. "But thankfully we still have some in the root cellar."

"What about the other things?" Liam asked.

"Well, let's see..." Tad looked over the field again. "The peas should be done in about eighty days, and the potatoes and corn in ninety."

They continued on, talking about the harvest. Then they put away their tools and went into the barn. After that, Tad and Liam went off to the smokehouse to stoke the fire, and Mary Elizabeth helped Gwyn separate the milk.

As they worked together, she talked on and on about all the things she and Tad had done together.

"You love your father, don't ye, child?" Gwyn asked.

"Oh yes!"

"You're a blessed girl to have such a father. He is a very good man."

"Yes," Mary Elizabeth responded. "He is, indeed."

"He's been mighty good to me and to Steffan," Gwyn said. "Mighty good."

"Tad is good to everyone," Mary Elizabeth explained. "I know it's because he loves the Lord. It shows in everything he does."

"Aye," Gwyn agreed, "and I know ye will grow into a young woman who loves the Lord just like your father."

They went on working side by side, but Mary Elizabeth couldn't stop thinking about all the things Gwyn had said. Every day she was more like her father, and every day she longed to be more like him still.

"There's nothing better than a tea party to use your prettiest things," Mam said, *"and I wanted to make this very special."*

TAKING TEA

*I*N EARLY JUNE, MAM DECIDED TO HOST a tea party for some of the ladies she had met in Virginia. The invitation list included Mrs. Morgan, Abby, Hope, Mrs. Anderson and Emma. For weeks, she and her mother planned this special event.

"For ladies only," Mam had whispered to Tad.

He just smiled and nodded.

When the big day arrived, Mary Elizabeth rushed downstairs to find Mam and Gwyn so that she could help. She located them in the parlor, where her mother was working hurriedly to prepare for today's event while Gwyn tended to the baby.

"Are ye nearly ready, daughter?" Mam turned to her with a smile.

"Oh yes! I'm so excited!"

"We will have several different kinds of teas," Mam explained, "since the ladies come from different places.

And Gwyn will have plenty of honey on hand from her honeybees."

Mary Elizabeth loved honey, but wasn't terribly fond of going with Gwyn to fetch it. The bees scared her a bit.

Mam continued on, telling about the party. "We will have cucumber sandwiches," she explained, "and I will serve scones and tea cakes, of course. Gwyn is nearly done baking the Apple Frictella now. We're going to have Bara Brith, naturally, along with some of Gwyn's wonderful biscuits with that delicious jam you helped me make from the blackberries you picked."

"Mmm." Mary Elizabeth could hardly wait. "What about the crabapple jelly? Can we have that too?"

"Aye," Mam said, "and the wild mulberry jelly as well. We will offer our guests many tasty treats." She smiled broadly. "Come and see the table."

Mam took the baby into her arms, and they walked out onto the back porch together. Mary Elizabeth gasped when she saw the beautiful outdoor table set with Mam's finest china and best silver. In the center of the table stood a large vase filled with fresh flowers.

"Oh, Mam! I had forgotten how pretty a table could look. I'm so happy that you used your best china dishes."

"There's nothing better than a tea party to use your prettiest things," Mam said, "and I wanted to make this very special."

"It will be special indeed."

"We have much to celebrate." Mam's eyes had a dreamy look. "Why, in less than a year we have sailed to Virginia, built a home, made it through the winter, harvested a crop, and brought a new life into the world."

Baby Virginia let out a little cry, and Mam leaned down to plant a soft kiss on her forehead. "What a blessed family we are."

"Yes," said Mary Elizabeth, giving her a warm hug. "We are blessed, for sure. And I love our new home. Don't you?"

"I do." Her mother looked up at the large grandfather clock, and turned to face her. "You'd best be getting dressed, Dearie. Why don't ye wear your lovely lavender dress?"

"My best dress we purchased in England?" Mary Elizabeth's eyes grew large. "Really?"

"Yes, of course. This is a very special occasion."

Mary Elizabeth quickly dressed in her beautiful lavender dress. Then she brushed her long brown curls and tied back part of her hair with a ribbon. She glided down the stairs, careful not to mess up her dress, to find her mam.

"I do believe our guests should be arriving soon," Mam said. "Let me go and see how Gwyn is coming with those tea cakes and Bara Brith."

She scurried off to the kitchen, putting Tad in charge of the baby. Mary Elizabeth followed along behind Mam to check on the food, and then the guests arrived in short order.

Abby met Mary Elizabeth with a squeal. "I'm so happy to be here, and you look so pretty!"

"Yes," Hope agreed. "You look quite grown-up, to be sure."

Mary Elizabeth gave a little twirl to show off her special dress. She looked at her friend's pretty pink dress and sighed. "You look beautiful, Abby!"

As Abby turned in a circle, the skirt on her soft pink dress floated out like a parasol.

Mrs. Morgan greeted Mam with a warm hug, and everyone chatted together until the Andersons arrived. Mary Elizabeth had waited for months to meet Emma, the daughter Mr. Anderson had told her about on their first trip from town. Emma was just about her age, and Mary Elizabeth was thrilled to find her very friendly.

Within moments, all the girls, along with their mothers, settled down at the table on the back porch.

"Everything is so lovely," Mrs. Morgan said.

"Yes, I don't know when I've seen such beautiful teacups," Mrs. Anderson agreed, picking up her cup to have a closer look.

"Thankfully, my china made the journey from Wales to Virginia without being broken," Mam said with a smile. "I'm so happy to have it, for it reminds me of home."

The women began to talk about their former homes—Mrs. Morgan telling a story about her house in England, Mrs. Anderson sharing a tale about her family in the English countryside, and Mam sharing a story about a visit to Laugharne Castle.

Mary Elizabeth listened intently, the stories so colorful she could almost see the places the ladies described. Then, as the women began to talk about other things, the girls turned their attention to one another.

"What is your favorite part about living in Virginia?" Mary Elizabeth asked Emma. After all, she had lived here the longest.

"I love the summertime," Emma said, "picnics out by the river, and the smell of wheat when it is harvested."

"Yes," Mary Elizabeth agreed. "This summer I have come to love that smell too."

"I love all the animals on the farm," Abby said. "We have chickens and roosters, and we have an ornery old cow named Beulah. Papa said she reminds him of a mule because of her stubbornness."

All the girls laughed.

"What do you love best, Mary Elizabeth?" Emma asked.

Mary Elizabeth thought for a moment before answering. "I love having a new baby sister, little Virginia. I also love sitting in the drawing room, listening to Tad read from his Bible. But most of all," she said, reaching across the table to squeeze the hands of both her friends, "I love my new friends. When we left Wales I was afraid I would be so lonely."

"I thought the same thing when I left London," Abby agreed.

"So did I," Hope said.

"Isn't it funny?" Mam gave Mrs. Morgan's hand a squeeze. "The Lord has brought us all from different places, and yet here we are—all together in one place. One beautiful, lovely place where we can worship God freely."

Mary Elizabeth leaned back against her chair as Gwyn served the tea cakes, thinking about what Mam had just said. The Lord had surely brought her from one place to another. No, she hadn't wanted to come, and there had been hard times along the way, to be sure. But now, as she looked into the eyes of her new friends, she realized that coming to this new land was, by far, the most wonderful thing that had ever happened to her. She would always thank God for bringing her here, and for the courage to persevere through the hard times.

What a wonderful year it had been, and what wonderful lessons she had learned along the way.

A LETTER TO A
FRIEND

Dear Alva,

I miss you so much. As I write this letter, it is now summertime here in Virginia. The house is built. It is lovely, with three rooms downstairs, and four above. I have never seen another like it. The Virginia territory is wild but beautiful. On a recent trip into town, I saw Indians for the first time, and I wasn't afraid. They were quite nice, in fact.

I have some wonderful news! Mam has had a baby! My new baby sister is named Virginia because that's where she was born. I love holding her and helping tend to her when she is crying.

The weather here is beautiful—Liam and I have a wonderful time running in the fields and picking berries, but we work hard too. I help Tad in the fields whenever he lets me. We harvested our first wheat crop a few weeks ago. You can't imagine how *much wheat we had, and every bit of it had to be thrashed by hand!*

I have learned to do so many things. I've made jams and jellies, and even learned to bake. I can shell peas and even milk the cow. Fortunately, Liam is better at that than I am. Tad says I'm good with the horses. I'm even learning to ride. Perhaps one day you will come, and I can teach you.

We have eaten some new foods here in Virginia that we didn't have in Wales. One is corn, which grows high on stalks. You have to shuck it to get to the kernels, which are golden yellow. It is wonderful cooked fresh from the garden, and you can also make some tasty dishes with it—johnnycakes, corn mush, and hasty pudding—but my favorite is fried slapjacks with molasses. It is ever so good.

There have been some hard times too. Winter was very difficult, and the wheat crop almost didn't make it. Liam fell in the river, and could have drowned, but Tad pulled him out. Tad says we must persevere, and I know he is right.

I love my new life here, but my heart hurts every time I think of you. I miss our days, playing in the meadow near Laugharne Castle, and I wonder if you have forgotten me. I hope not. I hope you will remember me always, as I will remember you. I pray for you and your family every day, and trust all is well. I wish you could come to Virginia to see us. Perhaps one day you will. The countryside is filling with more people every day, many of them from our homeland.

Please send me a letter when you can. It will take months to reach me, but I will cherish it with my life.

All my love, Mary Elizabeth Powell

P. S. Uncle Gaynor is engaged! He proposed to my tutor, Hope Morgan, on the evening of our tea party, and they will be married next month. I can hardly wait for the big day!

Mary Elizabeth lifted her quill and looked over what she had written. Satisfied, she folded the letter in half. She addressed it, and then she sealed it with Tad's ring seal—the one that had the family crest on it—pressing it into a melted bit of wax.

Afterwards, she leaned back in her chair with a smile. Had she really only been in Virginia one year? She could scarcely believe it. What a wonderful year it had been, and what wonderful lessons she had learned along the way.

With a happy smile on her face, she rose from her chair and skipped to the drawing room to find Tad.

*"Never forget, it's your faith
that will give you the courage to
persevere through every trial."*

PERSEVERANCE

ENNIFER JEAN LOOKED ACROSS THE TABLE at her grandmother, amazed by all she had heard. "How do you know this story, Grand Doll?"

Her grandmother's eyes lit up as she spoke. "My mother told me Mary Elizabeth's story when I was just about your age," she explained. "If I recall, she wanted me to hear it because I was struggling with perseverance."

"I understand," Jennifer Jean said, "and I'm glad you told us that story today."

Grand Doll looked across the table at all her grand-daughters. "You girls come from a long line of people who have persevered through many trials. Mary Elizabeth was just one example, but some of your own parents had to persevere as well." She paused to gaze at Jennifer Jean. "Did you realize that your father couldn't sing when he was a little boy?"

"What?" Jennifer Jean could hardly believe it. Why, her father had a wonderful singing voice.

"It's true," Grand Doll explained. "When he was young, a teacher once told him that he couldn't carry a tune in a bucket."

"What does that mean?" Holly asked.

"It means he couldn't sing on key. But you know what?"

"What?" All the girls asked at once.

Grand Doll grinned. "I told him he could sing if he would try and work hard enough—and he worked harder than ever to learn."

"He persevered!" Chelsea Marie said.

"Yes, indeed. Just like Mary Elizabeth. He went on to sing in his high school choir and in college. Why, he sang all around the world."

"Wow!" Kimberly Dawn and Rachel Ann said.

Grand Doll turned to face Jennifer Jean as she spoke the next words. "I wanted to tell you this story, especially, because I know what a hard time you're going through right now. I know it must seem like everything in your world is changing."

"Yes ma'am." Jennifer Jean felt tears rise up in her eyes and brushed them away.

"I just wanted to remind you that you have a strong constitution, just like Mary Elizabeth's father—and just like your own father. You can make it through this time, even if it's really hard."

"It *is* hard," Jennifer Jean said softly. "I don't want to move away. I don't want to leave everyone I know."

Grand Doll rose from the table and came around to where Jennifer Jean was seated. She reached down to give her a soft kiss on the cheek. "You are stronger than you think, and with the Lord's help, you will make it through this. Just hold fast to the scripture you heard in the story. Do you remember it?"

"It was from James, wasn't it?" Jennifer Jean asked.

"Yes. James chapter one, verse twelve. *Blessed is the man that endureth temptation: for when he is tried, he shall receive the crown of life, which the Lord hath promised to them that love him.*"

Jennifer Jean nodded. "I understand, Grand Doll. Thank you for reminding me."

For a moment no one spoke. Finally Grand Doll's eyes filled with tears and she bowed her head.

"What is it, Grand Doll?" Jennifer Jean asked. "What's wrong?"

"All this talk about perseverance has just reminded me of something in my own life."

"What's that?" Melanie Ann asked.

"I want you girls to know that I understand what it's like to go through hard times too. Every day I'm learning to persevere." Tears now landed on her wrinkled cheeks.

"What do you mean, Grand Doll?" Chelsea Marie asked.

"You girls have probably noticed that Poppie isn't himself lately. He hasn't been well, but we are persevering through that, and we will make it, with God's help."

The girls all nodded, and a couple even dabbed at their eyes with their napkins.

"We love you, Grand Doll," Holly said.

"And we will pray for Poppie," Sara Elizabeth added.

Jennifer Jean had just one more question, one she had to ask. "Grand Doll, the teapot we're using today... Is it really the very same one that Mary Elizabeth and her Mam used at *their* tea party?"

Her grandmother's beautiful eyes sparkled with joy as she answered. "That's right. The very same one."

Everyone grew silent as they stared at the little teapot with the pink rosebud on top.

"I'll tell you a little secret too." The girls all leaned in close as their grandmother spoke. "The doll I loaned you for the tea party—the one with the porcelain face? That's Alva, the very same doll Mary Elizabeth brought over to America on her journey from Wales."

"Oh, Grand Doll!" Jennifer Jean exclaimed.

I also have the wax ring seal that Mary Elizabeth used to seal her letter to Alva, if anyone is interested in seeing it."

"No way!" all the girls chorused.

Grand Doll nodded. "It's true. The memory trunk is full of a great many wonderful things." She paused for a moment, and then looked lovingly at all the girls. "So many valuable things have been passed down through the generations, but the greatest thing of all is the faith your parents, grandparents, and other relatives have shared with you. Never forget, it's your faith that will give you the courage to persevere through every trial."

The room suddenly grew noisy again as the little girls began to chatter merrily. Jennifer Jean didn't join in, not quite yet. Instead, she sat still for a moment, thinking about Mary Elizabeth and her journey from Wales to America.

"If Mary Elizabeth could persevere," Jennifer Jean whispered, "I know I can too."

With a smile on her face, she turned her attentions back to the tea party, ready to have the time of her life.

Fun Facts and More

§ "Tad" is the Welsh word for father.

§ "Mam" is the Welsh word for mother.

§ The Welsh people love music and still have a musical tradition called "Cymanfa Ganu: Hymn Singing."

§ The Welsh language is a "Celtic" language that is still spoken today.

§ The real name of the *Assurance* was *Assurance de lo*. This ship actually sailed from England to Virginia in 1635.

§ Most people who came to America in the 1600s traveled two or three months by ship to get here.

§ Many people came to America for religious freedom, but others came because they heard that America was a "land of milk and honey." They hoped to become wealthy in America.

§ The first colony was in Jamestown, Virginia (not far from the Isle of Wight) and was settled in 1607.

§ The Isle of Wight is one of Virginia's eight original shires. A shire is similar to a county. Since its county government was established in 1634, it is one of the oldest county governments in the United States.

§ The Isle of Wight boasts one of the oldest Protestant churches in America, which is believed to have been built in 1632. It is referred to as the Old Brick Church, but it is also called St. Lukes Church or Benns Church.

§ On August 24, 1635 (about one month after the Powells landed in Virginia), the first historical reference to a major hurricane affecting the Virginia coast is recorded.

§ In 1587, the first English child to be born in North America was named Virginia Dare.

§ The Bible Tad read out of would have probably been the King James Version of the Bible. It was composed by a committee of English scholars and completed in 1611.

§ Indentured servants were people who wanted to come to America, but couldn't afford passage aboard a ship. Others would pay their way, then provide food and lodging for that person in exchange for work for a certain period of time.

Questions to Ponder

§ What does it mean to persevere? When was the last time you had to persevere?

§ Can you relate to Jennifer's Jean's struggle? Have you ever had to persevere through something as difficult as the divorce of your parents?

§ What would it be like to leave your home and travel halfway across the world like Mary Elizabeth and her family did?

§ Can you guess what the word "buccaneer" means?

§ What would be the hardest thing about living in 1635? What would be the best thing?

§ If you could choose between living in Virginia and living in Wales, which would you choose?

§ How do the chores Mary Elizabeth and Liam performed around the farm compare to your chores?

§ Have you ever been to a tea party? If so, what was it like?

§ What were some of Mary Elizabeth's favorite foods, and what are some of your favorite foods? How are they alike? How are they different?

§ How was Mary Elizabeth's schooling different
from yours?

§ Mary Elizabeth was good with horses. What animals
do you enjoy?

What Is Perseverance?

*W*EBSTER'S DICTIONARY DEFINES *perseverance* like this: "to persist (keep on) ... in spite of opposition, or discouragement (difficulties)."[1]

There are many scriptures in the Bible that speak about perseverance. One in particular is found in Romans 5:3–4 (NKJV): *And not only that, but we also glory in tribulations* [difficulties], *knowing that tribulation* [difficulty] *produces perseverance; and perseverance, character; and character, hope.*

But what does perseverance look like to us? How can we apply it to our lives? Listed are some simple descriptions of perseverance.

1. Keep on doing what you know is right until you reach your goal.
2. Don't give up on yourself.

---

[1] *Merriam Webster's Collegiate Dictionary*, 11th Edition, s.v. "Persevere."

3. Keep on doing the right thing even when you have difficulties.

4. Keep on trying even when you fail. A "failure" is not someone who fails. A "failure" is someone who gives up when the going gets tough.

The Bible tells of many people who had to persevere through times of trouble. One such person was Joseph in the Old Testament. Joseph had a dream that was given to him by God himself, but he had to go through many years of trials until that dream came true. His first trial was being rejected by his brothers, sold as a slave, and taken to a foreign land. Yet even in his slavery, he persevered with honor and strength of character, and he was elevated to head of his master's household. His trials were not over; however, for he was falsely accused and thrown into prison. Yet Joseph did not give up on himself or God. Even in prison, he was given a place of authority, and God blessed him. Joseph persevered in prison until he was used to interpret the dreams of Pharaoh himself. Pharaoh saw in him what others also saw: perseverance, honor, and the hand of God. In God's time, Joseph was then placed in the position God had for him all along—although he did not get there quickly or easily. He had to trust God and His promises and persevere through many trials. Joseph had to make a decision every time he was faced with difficulties. He chose to persevere and trust God for the dream that God had given him.

And also if anyone competes in athletics, he is not crowned unless he competes according to the rules (2 Timothy 2:5 NKJV). It has been said that "the victor receives the crown." A victor is someone who has won something…a race, a prize, a crown. A victor is also someone who never gives up and keeps on going until he reaches the goal or crosses the finish line. Have you ever been in a race but came in last or close to it? Did you give up and quit trying? Or did you try again? If you practiced and kept trying, you may have finished in a better position like third, second, or even first. Determined to win, you kept on until you won the prize. That's perseverance. Paul says in Hebrews 12:1-2 (NKJV): …*let us run with endurance* [perseverance] *the race that is set before us, looking unto Jesus, the author and finisher of our faith, who for the joy that was set before Him endured the cross, despising the shame, and has sat down at the right hand of the throne of God.* Perseverance means having endurance.

Perseverance is being faithful to a friend even when they have hurt you. It is doing what is right over and over again, even if the friend turns his back on you. Can you think of a time when this has happened to you? How did you respond? Did you keep on being faithful and try to make things right? God rewards the faithful with blessings. *A faithful man* [woman or child] *will abound with blessings…* (Proverbs 28:20 NKJV).

Perseverance is doing a good job for your parents and teachers even when they don't notice. It is pressing on when it gets hard and you want to quit. It is keeping at it until you succeed in doing the job well. Do you work hard and try to do your best even when no one else is around to see you? Do you finish a task that was assigned to you with excellence? Does it make you happy when you succeed, even when you don't get praised for it? Remember, even if no one else on earth sees you, God does.

> *For the ways of man are before the eyes of the* LORD, *and He ponders* [observes or sees] *all his paths* [the way he walks or behaves] (Proverbs 5:21 NKJV).

§   How did the characters in this story persevere? Can you give some examples?

_____

_____

_____

_____

_____

§   Is there anyone you know (family or friend) who has had to persevere?

_____

_____

_____

_____

_____

§ List at least three areas in your own life where you
   can use perseverance (such as school, family problems, relationships):

_____

_____

_____

_____

_____

"Be of good cheer. Do not think of today's failures,
but of the success that may come tomorrow. You have
set yourselves a difficult task, but you will succeed if you

persevere; and you will find a joy in overcoming obstacles. Remember, no effort that we make to attain something beautiful is ever lost."[2]

This is a quote from Helen Keller who had to endure a lifetime of trials. Have you ever read a book about Helen Keller? If you haven't, she is a good example of what it means to persevere. Read about her, and you will see what perseverance is really about.

Blessed is the man who endures [perseveres] *temptation; for when he has been approved, he will receive the crown of life which the Lord has promised to those who love Him* (James 1:12 NKJV).

Godly perseverance
never gives up!

---

[2] *The Book of Positive Quotations*, Compiled by John Cook, (New York: Random House, Grammercy Books, 1999), 495.

Taking Tea

MANY YOUNG LADIES IN OLDEN DAYS called a tea party "Taking Tea." That may sound strange to us, but that was the custom then. Today our tea parties may be nothing like what the girls in the past experienced. Theirs were somewhat formal and had many "rules of etiquette" they followed as they "took" their tea. We can look back at the past and recreate it, learn some good manners from those times, and have fun in the process. Here is what it may have looked like back then.

The tea was usually served in a special room in the home—say a dining room or what they called a "parlor" or "drawing room." The table was covered with a beautiful white lace or linen tablecloth, and there was a vase of fresh flowers on the table. Each place setting was usually a matched set of fine china; the "Victorian Rose" pattern being one of the most popular. It included a small dessert plate, a tea cup and saucer, a fork, spoon, butter knife, and a lovely little linen napkin.

The food choices were served on a pedestal-type serving dish. The dish held a variety of treats such as scones, shortbread, fresh fruit, and an assortment of small sandwiches...without the crusts, of course! We can't have crusts at a tea party, can we? Sweet little cakes, called "tea cakes," with roses or other decorations on top, were also served.

Sugar, lemon, and cream were served to "dress" the tea; the cream used was called "clotted" (or heavy) cream. A beautiful, floral teapot was filled with very hot water and covered with what is called a "tea cozy." That's a very funny name, don't you think? It is called that because of its purpose...to keep the teapot warm and "cozy." Back then the tea was very different from what is mostly served in our day. It was loose tea leaves instead of tea bags. There may have been several different flavors to choose from, and each girl made her choice before her tea was poured. Oh, and there was also a tea strainer at each place setting so the leaves wouldn't fall into the tea cups. This strainer was placed on top of the cup, filled with the tea of choice, and then the hot water was poured over it to make the tea. Now that we've set the scene for the tea, let's look at the way the "ceremony" was carried out.

When the young ladies received the "Invitation to Tea" either by mail or special messenger, they accepted by sending back a written note to say thank you. Then, on the day of the tea, the excitement began as they chose what they would wear. Each girl probably wore a favorite dress that was used mainly for church or other special occasions. She wore a very feminine hat and carried a dainty pair of white gloves.

As soon as all the girls arrived at the party, after thanking their hostess for the invitation, they were shown to their places at the table, which were marked with place cards with their names. That was probably a memory they took home with them to place in their journals. After being seated, each girl unfolded her napkin and placed it on her lap. Then the tea party began.

At that point, if the girls didn't already know one another, they were getting acquainted. There was probably a lot of giggling going on around the table as the fun progressed. As they chatted about the exciting things happening in each of their lives, they chose their tea. The hostess then had each girl pass her teacup to her to be filled, asking, "Do you prefer sugar, lemon, or cream?" That may sound a bit formal to you, but don't let that prevent you from doing it—politeness never goes out of style. Then the treats were passed around the table from left to right. None of the girls began eating until everyone had been served because to do so was considered rude behavior.

The time flew by as the girls chatted, giggled, and shared their lives with one another—all a part of "taking their tea." Before leaving the home, each guest left her "calling card" for the hostess, letting her know that the guest would like to return the favor.

"Taking Tea" was seen as a time for practicing good manners and politeness as the girls were becoming young ladies. It was a learning experience that prepared them to hostess their own tea parties one day.

DISCOVER THE FUN AND ADVENTURE of preparing to hostess your very own tea party. You will learn how easy and fun it can be when you practice "The Art of Taking Tea." That's right. Just think of it as fun, creative, and artistic. Let your imagination create a setting that will be pleasing to both you and your guests.

PICK OUT A THEME

Traditional Party: This is where everyone arrives for the party in their favorite frilly dress, complete with hat and gloves.

Dress-Up Party: Invite everyone to dress up in their mom's or older sister's prom dresses, along with some fancy jewelry.

Garden Party: When the weather is good, you can plan a party outdoors. Set up a table in the yard or patio, and garnish it with a lot of fresh flowers and greenery.

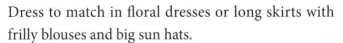

Dress to match in floral dresses or long skirts with frilly blouses and big sun hats.

Setting From a Favorite Novel: *Anne of Green Gables* (imagine her farmhouse and its setting), *Little Women* (recreate a scene from the book), *Gone with the Wind* (dress up as southern belles), etc.

Holiday Tea Parties: Plan a tea party around one of your favorite holidays, such as Christmas or Valentine's Day.

PLAN AHEAD

1. Select a date and time.
2. Make a list of the girls you wish to invite, keeping in mind the size of your room and the table or tables you will use. Limiting the number to 4 to 8 girls would be wise.
3. Shop for invitations to mail out, or invite by telephone or e-mail.
4. Mail invitations, telephone, or e-mail at least two weeks before the party.
5. After receiving replies, plan how you will set up your room.
6. Make name cards for each girl who will be attending.
7. Decide on your menu and buy all the necessary ingredients. Plan on several different types of tea

sandwiches and have a variety of desserts. Fresh fruit is also a nice addition to your menu. (If you don't wish to bake, purchase dessert items from a store or bakery.)

8. Make sure you have a good selection of teas.

THE DAY BEFORE THE PARTY

1. Clean the room you will be using and be sure to get all those "dust bunnies."
2. Wash and iron (if needed) the tablecloth and napkins.
3. Wash and dry your tea set, dishes, and silverware.
4. Bake your desserts and place in airtight containers.
5. Make sandwiches (remember, no crusts allowed) and place in a plastic container with waxed paper between the layers. Put a slightly damp linen tea towel or paper towel on the top, seal, and place in the refrigerator.

THE DAY OF THE PARTY

1. Set your table (or tables) with a tablecloth, a bouquet of fresh flowers, a bowl of sugar cubes, slices of lemon, and a pitcher of cream.

2. Place a dessert plate, teacup and saucer, tea strainer, napkin, and silverware at each place setting. (Napkin to the left of plate with the fork on top and place knife and spoon to the right). Also, put each girl's name card just above her dessert plate.

3. Put the number of chairs you will use around the table or tables.

4. Remove the sandwiches from the refrigerator about one hour before the party.

5. About 30 minutes before your guests arrive, put your desserts and sandwiches on serving plates and place a selection at each table.

6. Get yourself dressed according to the theme you have chosen.

7. As the girls arrive, invite them in and thank them for coming.

8. Show them to your "Tea Room," and invite them to visit with one another until all the girls arrive.

9. After everyone arrives, have them find their places.

10. Let each one choose her tea.

11. As hostess, if you have a tea cart, you can ask each one to pass her cup so you can pour the hot water over her tea and return the cup to her, or each table can have a teapot of hot water and a volunteer can be in charge of serving the tea for their table.

12. As each table will have the cream, sugar, and lemon on it, a polite, "Please pass the cream, lemon, or sugar" is encouraged.

13. As you help yourselves to the sandwiches and desserts, remembering to pass from the left to the right, be sure to wait until all the girls at your table have been served before you begin eating…only good manners will do. Pray a blessing before you begin.

14. Now, I suppose, the rest is up to you. Tea time is slowing down and enjoying the moment, catching up with good friends, and meeting new ones.

ENDING THE PARTY

As each girl leaves, she may want to extend an informal invitation to hostess a Tea at her home in the near future. Maybe you could suggest forming a club that meets once a month at each of your friend's homes. Tea parties are a great time to practice good manners and meet new friends.

Take time for tea…
it's good for the soul.

Bread (white, wheat, or raisin)
Butter for spreading
Sandwich fillings:
    Chicken salad
    Tuna salad
    Pimento cheese spread
    Cream cheese and jam
    Cucumber and cream cheese

Chicken salad, tuna salad, and pimento cheese

Take two slices of bread and, using a butter knife, spread both slices of bread with a small amount of soft butter. Then, on one slice, spread chicken salad, tuna salad, or pimento cheese generously. Place the other slice of buttered bread on top of the filling and press together gently.

Take a sharp knife (ask your mom to help you with this) and cut off the crusts. Then cut the sandwich across one way, turn and cut across the other way, making 4 triangle tea sandwiches.

CREAM CHEESE AND JAM

Take two slices of bread and, using a butter knife, spread one slice of bread with softened cream cheese. On the other slice of bread, spread about one tablespoon of strawberry or raspberry jam. Put the slices together and press gently.

Take a sharp knife (ask your mom to help you) and cut off the crusts. Then cut the sandwich across one way, turn and cut across the other way, making 4 triangle tea sandwiches.

CUCUMBER AND CREAM CHEESE

4 ounce package of cream cheese, softened
2 tablespoons chopped chives (optional)
1 cucumber, sliced into thin rounds

Mix chives into the softened cream cheese. Spread one side of bread with cream cheese. Top with 2-3 slices of cucumber. Spread cream cheese on the other slice of bread and put slices together. Press gently.

Take a sharp knife (ask your mom to help you) and cut off the crusts. Then cut the sandwich across one way, turn and cut across the other way, making 4 triangle tea sandwiches.

VARIATION

In addition to triangle tea sandwiches, you can use cookie cutters to make decorative sandwiches. Use your cookie cutter and cut out the center of several slices of bread. Remove the crusts. Follow instructions above for adding different sandwich fillings.

Store sandwiches in a waxed paper-lined plastic container with slightly damp paper towels between the layers and on top. Seal tightly and place in refrigerator until time to serve.

Easy Tea
Cakes

1 cup butter (softened)
2 1/4 cups all purpose flour
1/2 cup powdered sugar
1 teaspoon vanilla
1/4 teaspoon salt
1/4 cup powdered sugar

❑ Preheat oven to 400 degrees.
❑ Spray coat cookie sheet.
❑ Put butter in large mixing bowl and cream with a mixer. Add flour, sugar, vanilla, and salt. Mix until dough is fairly stiff.
❑ Chill in refrigerator for one to two hours.
❑ Remove from refrigerator and roll into small balls (about one inch).
❑ Place on cookie sheet and bake for 14–17 minutes.
❑ Remove from cookie sheet and roll in powdered sugar.
❑ Cool on a wire rack and roll in powdered sugar again.

Butter Scones

2 cups all purpose flour

4 tablespoons sugar

2 teaspoons baking powder

1/2 teaspoon salt

6 tablespoons butter (softened)

2 eggs (beaten)

1/2 cup sour cream

1/2 teaspoon vanilla

❑ Preheat oven to 375 degrees.

❑ Spray coat one 8-inch round cake pan and a cookie sheet.

❑ In a large mixing bowl, combine flour, sugar, baking powder, and salt. Mix in the butter with a pastry blender until mixture resembles coarse meal.

❑ In a separate bowl, combine the eggs, sour cream, and vanilla and mix well.

❑ Add egg mixture to the flour mixture and stir until combined.

❑ Shape the dough into a circle. With flour on your hands, lightly press the dough into an 8-inch round cake pan. After dough is lightly pressed, take a knife and loosen dough from edge of pan.

❑ Turn cake pan upside down onto a baking sheet to remove dough from the pan and onto the baking sheet. (You might need to tap back of pan several times to remove dough.)

❑ Score rounded dough (not cut through) with a knife into 8 or 16 wedges.

❑ Bake for 18–20 minutes until lightly browned and inserted toothpick comes out clean.

❑ Remove from oven. Cut wedges completely through and place on a wire rack to cool slightly (1–2 minutes). Place wedges on a serving plate and dust with powdered sugar.

Best served warm with butter, preserves, or honey.

The Eleanor
Series

LEANOR CLARK CONCEIVED THE IDEA
for *The Eleanor Series* while researching her
family's rich American history. Motivated
by her family lineage, which had been traced back to the
early 17th century, a God-ordained idea emerged: the
legacy left by her ancestors provided the perfect tool to
reach today's children with the timeless truths of patri-
otism, godly character, and miracles of faith. Through
her own family's stories, she instills in children a love of
God and country, along with a passion for history. With
that in mind, she set out to craft this collection of novels
for the youth of today. Each story in *The Eleanor Series*
focuses on a particular character trait, and is laced with
the pioneering spirit of one of Eleanor's true-to-life family
members. These captivating stories span generations, are
historically accurate, and highlight the nation's Christian
heritage of faith. Twenty-first century readers—both
children and parents—are sure to relate to these amazing
character-building stories of young American's while
learning Christian values and American history.

LOOK FOR ALL OF THESE BOOKS IN THE ELEANOR SERIES:

Christmas Book—*Eleanor Jo: A Christmas to Remember*
ISBN-10: 0-9753036-6-X
ISBN-13: 978-0-9753036-6-5

Available in 2007

Book One—*Mary Elizabeth: Welcome to America*
ISBN-10: 0-9753036-7-8
ISBN-13: 978-0-9753036-7-2

Book Two—*Victoria Grace: Courageous Patriot*
ISBN-10: 0-9753036-8-6
ISBN-13: 978-0-9753036-8-9

Book Three—*Katie Sue: Heading West*
ISBN-10: 0-9788726-0-6
ISBN-13: 978-0-9788726-0-1

Book Four—*Sarah Jane: Liberty's Torch*
ISBN-10: 0-9753036-9-4
ISBN-13: 978-0-9753036-9-6

Book Five—*Eleanor Jo: The Farmer's Daughter*
ISBN-10: 0-9788726-1-4
ISBN-13: 978-0-9788726-1-8

Book Six—*Melanie Ann: A Legacy of Love*
ISBN-10: 0-9788726-2-2
ISBN-13: 978-0-9788726-2-5

Visit our Web site at: www.eleanorseries.com

About the Author

LEANOR CLARK LIVES IN central Texas with Lee, her husband of over 50 years, and as matriarch of the family, she is devoted to her 5 children, 17 grandchildren, and 4 great grandchildren.

Born the daughter of a Texas sharecropper and raised in the Great Depression, Eleanor was a female pioneer in crossing economic, gender, educational, and corporate barriers. An executive for one of America's most prestigious ministries, Eleanor later founded her own highly successful consulting firm. Her appreciation of her American and Christian heritage comes to life along with her exciting and colorful family history in the youth fiction series, *The Eleanor Series.*